Pass the Butter
Book 3 in the series
The Life and Times of Amelia Ciracco

By Nikki DiCaro

Nikki DiCaro

Pass the Butter

Pass the Butter
Book Three in the Series: *The Life and Times of Amelia Ciracco*
By Nikki DiCaro

Copyright © 2019 Nikki DiCaro – All Rights Reserved

The following is a work of fiction. Names, characters, businesses, places, events and incidents are either the products of the author's imagination or used in a fictitious manner. Any resemblance to actual persons, living or dead, or actual events is purely coincidental.

No part of this book may be used or reproduced in any manner whatsoever without the written permission of the author except in the case of brief quotations embodied in critical articles and reviews.

Nikki can be reached by email at: Nikki@DiCaro1.com.

Nikki also writes Thrillers under the pen name D.D. Nicaro. You can you can preview her first four Thrillers as well as other book by Nikki at www.NikkiDiCaro.com

Nikki DiCaro

Pets

"Mom, can we have a dog?" Why do kids always ask mom? Because dads say, "Ask your mother," and walk away absolved of all decision-making responsibility. This is how things started. Somebody put the bug in my middle daughter's brain. *A dog, really?* She asked me at a moment of weakness. If clairvoyants have a special ability to see things, kids have the innate ability to sense weakness. Does it come from our roots in the animal kingdom? Wherever it originated, kids are thick with it. They know; and parents know too but we're too silly over our kids to disappoint them. Dogs are man's best friend, right? I thought it was the remote control, followed closely by bottled beer and sex. Woman's best friend varied based upon the time of day and day of the month!

A dog didn't sound like a bad idea. Family portraits leaned towards dogs; the all-American family. Why else would I agree to bring another living thing into this crazy house of a home? Three kids, husband and me. Dog makes an even half dozen.

"Who's gonna take care of it?" I asked, trying to sound noncommittal.

"It's not an *it*. It's a girl or a boy dog." A girl or boy? Talk about being sensitive. At seven Lisa had manipulation down to a science. I felt bad about being insensitive towards an animal we hadn't yet purchased.

"Why do you think a dog would want to come live in our home?" I continued, "Who's going to take care of the dog?" I asked again, sidestepping the gender thing.

"We love dogs," the three conspirators replied in stereo.

"I'll take care of the dog," Lisa said with one of her innocent smiles that held no understanding of the consequences.

"And we'll help," the other two added.

"Do you know what it means to take care of the dog?" I asked contemplating walks in the rain and snow, paw prints all over my clean floors and pet hair on the furniture and in the carpets. This wasn't helping. "Pets are a big responsibility." I continued, as if any of this was registering. Lisa, the designated representative, offered another little girl smile taking an emotional pry bar to my resistance.

"I'll walk him," she said, expecting me to believe it. How many parents heard words of commitment from children thrilled by the thought of a pet only to be relegated to caretaker of the family mutt? Lisa's attention span was already microscopic. I didn't see a high-maintenance pet lengthening it.

"When it snows and rains? Before school and after school?"

"Yes," came the response without a moment's thought. I believed that just like I believed in happy endings, Santa Claus and the Easter Bunny.

"I don't think a dog's a good idea." This brought a pout and tears. She could bring rain at the drop of a hat. Native Americans (can't call them Indians without threats of lawsuits) should be so successful. My little drama queen. I thought about the devastation she might deliver to the men in her adult life.

"Let me talk with dad."

"He said it's okay with him if it's okay with you." She had already breached that fortress of resolve, hah! This was going to require finesse. Was there a store that sold finesse because I was fresh out.

"I have to think about it and I still want to talk with dad."

Pass the Butter

"Okay," she said bopping away like the cat that ate the canary; followed by her partners in crime yet to be perpetrated. Did I just lose a decision to a seven-year-old? The thought nagged me. Did Ralph already give his contingent blessing? Standing in the middle of the kitchen I looked around trying to remember what I was doing before my daughter and her cohorts blind-sided me.

Would a pet be a bad thing? I've heard about the benefits of a dog. We would get into the habit of walking three times a day. Warm sunny days, a smile on my face and a spring in my step. I was hallucinating. The walks would happen in the dark in the mornings and evenings when it was cold and rainy. Drying off the dog's paws and fur otherwise he or she would shake all the water out of its fur and spray it around the house.

About those walks, you can't leave dog droppings – pet waste as it's called on signs posted around the neighborhood – you have to pick them up. Warm poop, hopefully solid enough to pick up in little plastic bags. It sounded so wrong.

Dear lady, would you mind retrieving that pile? I'd pick it up but I don't have fingers or opposable thumbs. We wouldn't want to violate the local ordinances, would we?

The register was coming up 'no sale' on the dog. Remembering why I was in the kitchen I washed the rest of the dishes in the sink. The dishwasher was full and needed to be run. I dropped a drinking glass in the sink and it cracked. "Shit!" The whole pet thing had me distracted. Tossing the broken pieces, focusing to keep from cutting myself, I dried my hands and walked into the living room. If I didn't clear my head I was going be consumed by this thing. Checking the clock on the wall above the piano in the dining room, Ralph should have been home from golf. He and my dad were usually finished by 3 p.m. I needed to talk this ten plus year commitment through. If we were going to make this decision we were going to make it together.

Let's see, which neighbors have dogs? The Murphys have a Golden Retriever. That dog leaves big piles. Again l the thought of picking up warm terds did nothing to make me feel better. The Giordanos have two terriers. Those dogs barked a lot. *How do you stop a dog from barking? Don't buy one.* I laughed at myself. The Francos have a collie. That was a beautiful dog. Looks like Lassie. Did you know Lassie was a female? *Probably leaves lots of hair all over the place.* I tried to remember the last time I was over their house. Come to think of it we haven't been to their place for a while but they kept coming here. Reminder to self – what to do about the Francos. There were a few other dogs in the neighborhood but I couldn't remember the breed or who owned them.

I wasn't getting the warms and fuzzies about a pet. Veterinary bills, flea and tick medicine, ringworm, heartworm, roundworm and all the other worms. This was going to be expensive Besides all the other stuff, who was going to house train it? More thoughts of brown droppings and yellow-stained wet newspaper; clean up and disinfecting. This was becoming a refusal-fest. Lisa wasn't going to like the decision.

By 5 p.m. Ralph rolled in. The guys had been drinking, surprise! Drinking and driving; another pet peeve of mine. He was frisky and playful. I indulged him until I couldn't take the beer and hot dog breath mixture. "Brush your teeth, and use mouthwash. You know I don't like kissing a beer mouth." He tried one more time. "Go, now! The kids will be in for dinner and I don't want them smelling alcohol on you. While you're up there, take a shower and maybe we'll have adult playtime when the kids go to bed." The promise of a little under cover action got him moving. We had things to discuss and I needed him focused on something other than his libido.

The kids ate and helped clean up. It's never too late to get them involved in household things. They didn't seem to mind. The kitchen was in order; meaning I could relax.

Pass the Butter

"Did you talk with dad? Can we have a dog?"

"Not yet honey. I'll talk to him tonight." She hugged me tightly; her form of bribery. I began to understand how hard it was to say no to a child. She was not going to relent. Her pressure was subtle and she knew it. I'd like to know where she learned it. I don't remember being manipulative when I was Lisa's age. Times were different. My parents were supportive but not without their monarchical approach to decisions.

The kids were playing a board game at the kitchen table. Laughter mixed with a few complaints and threats like, "I'm gonna tell mom you're cheating" found their way to my ears.

"Glad you're the referee," Ralph said.

"I'll give them a few minutes. If things get out of control I'll go and tell them "your father's going to come in here!" He kissed my hand then bit my forearm playfully.

"What's this about a dog?"

"Lisa approached me; more like assaulted me – one of *your* outflank maneuvers." Before I finished the sentence the kids swooped in like a tornado.

"Please, please can we have a dog, can we?" They must have been practicing because the plead came in three-speaker stereo. Lisa climbed into her father's lap. He was toast. Suzanne and Randy bookended me on the sofa.

"If I could only get you to be so loving when I ask you to do something."

"We will, we will. We promise." More stereo.

"What kind of dog are you thinking?" Ralph's question stopped all the theatrics. "You don't know what kind of dog?"

Lisa said, "A little one."

Randy said, "A big one."

Suzanne said, "I don't care, I just want a dog."

"Who's going to take care of the dog?" Three hands shot up.

"The dog can sleep in my bed."

"No in mine."

"Hey, in my bed." The wrangling commenced. Ralph had a knack for tossing live grenades into a crowd and watching the commotion.

"Time out!" I had to step in. Hubby wasn't helping matters. In hindsight he was probably doing the right thing. His questions churned up a bunch more questions sure to buy us some time. I was resigning myself to the fact we were going to lose this one. If we played it right, we might be able to use the pet experience as a way to build responsibility in small portions. *Sure, and if that didn't work, mom could start an anti-psychotic drug regimen.*

This wasn't the first time a pet had come up. Ralph talked pets before I got pregnant with Suzanne. With the baby on the way I earned at least a temporary reprieve. Before you ask, I didn't get pregnant like clockwork to keep from getting a dog. I wasn't ready for another mouth to feed along with all the complications a pet brings.

The pet saga quieted after a couple of days. There were straggler questions about breeds. Pictures of dogs cut out of magazines were left on the coffee table and kitchen table with a hand-drawn heart and the name of the informant. I filed the pictures in the collection drawer in the kitchen. I didn't have the heart to toss them. Ralph laughed when I shared the pictures.

"They are relentless. Like you when you want something!" I acted offended and pinched his arm.

"I am not relentless!"

"If you say so." His way of dismissing a counterargument.

"Tell me one time when I was relentless." He gave me one of those "if you think I'm dumb enough to answer that question, keep thinking' looks.

"Do you really think a pet is a good idea?" I didn't want to rain on the kids' parade.

"I had one; Buddy was great. Lived twelve years; about the average life span for the breed."

"Tell me about Buddy." I couldn't believe I was headed down that rabbit hole.

"Border Collie. Also called Shetland Sheep Dog. He was a herder. Full of energy and smart as a whip." I think my question touched an emotional nerve.

"Hard to train?"

"Nope, learned in a week or so. Really didn't seem like it took that long. We got him when he was almost small enough to fit in my hands. Probably twenty pounds fully grown." I started calculating dog food, grooming, droppings, etc. Didn't sound unmanageable.

"If we got a dog, and I'm not saying I'm on board, which breed would you choose?" The kids cut out pictures of everything from little dogs to big dogs. I knew exactly zero about dogs. We had a cat when I was growing up; my mother claimed it helped her deal with all the miscarriages. I started calling it 'doctor cat'. I'm not a cat person. I don't do litter boxes and I don't like my furniture torn to shreds.

"Small dog would be best. Sheltie would be my preference."

"They're like miniature collies, right? What about the hair?"

"Requires regular brushing and bathing. Buddy loved being groomed and didn't mind baths." I'm imagining myself giving this dog a bath and brushing its coat. *I don't brush my hair enough and I'm going to brush the dog?*

"Could be a good thing for the kids. Buddy was a big part of the family."

"How did it go when he died?" I had to know; figuring one of us would be taking care of final arrangements.

"Not well. I was sixteen when he died. Struggled with it; like losing my best friend." *Great! More drama.* Doing the calculations, Suzanne would be twenty-one, Lisa, nineteen and Randy seventeen if the dog lived twelve years.

"You want a dog, don't you?" I asked. I couldn't leave it alone. You understand the whole inquiring minds thing.

"I wouldn't mind."

"You'd work to make sure the kids took care of the dog?"

"Sure."

"What about the dog being home alone all day. Your mom didn't work, so Buddy had company."

"Mom didn't want the dog. Dad brought it home without warning. One of his friends at work had puppies from their pure bred." He stopped, suddenly lost in thought. "Mom never let dad live it down." That explained a lot. I wasn't crazy about how this conversation turned around. I was the wicked witch in this scene. If I said okay I'd be taking on something I knew nothing about. If I said no, I'd have to deal with the fallout. I couldn't ask Ralph to take the fall for it. He already coated himself in Teflon by abdicating the decision to me. *Do I let my kids down or do I suck it up?*

"You think the dog would be okay home alone?"

"We get a kennel cage. It can stay in there until we're comfortable with letting it have the run of the house. We can put up a gate to keep the dog downstairs or put the dog in the basement." All these conditions were making me dizzy. We went through the 'gates' phase when the kids were little. Did I want to dog-proof the house like we child-proofed the house?

"I don't know how I feel about keeping the dog caged all day."

"You're just a softie," he said, kissing me in that way; marking the official end to discussions and the beginning of sex. *Maybe we should talk more because he was... oh God! Oh God!*

Pass the Butter

Roxy

Roxy sniffed around the house; enthralled with her new surroundings. She was a tiny, ball of fur, Sheltie. The mother of one of Lisa's classmates bred her Sheltie and Roxy was the only female in a litter of nine. I realized the 'dog thing' wasn't confined only to my family. I think Lisa knew this was happening and she was setting us up. Kids conspired to get their way.

The name was 'Roxy' had been decided a week before the dog appeared. The three conspirators had jumped right over acquisition to naming. The decision was by majority vote. Suzanne was the dissenter but I don't think she really cared. Randy was sweet to let Lisa win. I think it was the spoils for her carrying the battle to us and winning.

Brown tones with large white chest and underbelly. She was cute. It didn't take long for me to warm to her. The kids were wild about her. Watching them made the decision feel right. I understood this was the honeymoon period and when newness wore of it would be back to the usual. I hoped Ralph was right; Roxy would make an impact and the kids would bond with her.

The first two weeks were challenging. She came to us practically from the womb. She was six weeks old and had no knowledge of anything dog except eating, sleeping, peeing, pooping and chewing on her toys. We did the 'newspaper on the kitchen floor' thing. We walked her several times a day and she did very little in the house. We kept the kennel in the family room with the door open. There was a soft used blanket on the bottom and each kid surrendered a stuffed animal to the kennel. That didn't last long. Roxy mauled one of them until the stuffing was showing. So much for that idea. We promptly removed the other animals before they suffered the same fate. It wasn't the dog's fault. She hadn't the opportunity to read Adopted Dog Weekly.

For the first two weeks she slept in the wire kennel. "Don't call it a cage, that's for wild animals. Roxy is a member of the family," Suzanne chided. A member of the family, huh? This lasted two weeks because it wasn't going to survive one day longer. My head must have been someplace else when I decided to keep the dog downstairs while we slept on the second floor. She whined, whimpered and barked most of the night – separation anxiety. She had been taken from her mother when she was barely weaned. When I finally came to my senses, we moved the kennel to Lisa's bedroom. Roxy settled down.

A week later we trusted her enough to sleep with the kids. They fought for the right to have her. Our diabolical plan of creating responsibility was working! The puppy had a few drawbacks. She was tiny and wasn't able to climb and descend the stairs. She couldn't get up or down from the bed without help. Could dogs suffer hydrophobia? Nothing would surprise me.

Walking her was interesting. She bristled against the leash. It took longer to get her accustomed to the leash than to train her about bathroom things. She even took to sleeping in her kennel during the day. We kept it in a corner of the family room with the door open and a comfortable blanket on its floor along with one of her favorite doggie toys.

Pass the Butter

Late winter snow blanketed the neighborhood; enough to cancel school. This was the first snow day of the year and even I welcomed the opportunity to work from home. Not much work got done with three kids and a dog to contend with. We did have a snowball fight in the yard and enjoyed watching our little fur ball bound around in the powdery white stuff. Roxy didn't seem to mind. The kids chased her and eventually they collapsed in balls of laughter over the dog's antics. She was a sheep herding dog, hence the breed Shetland Sheep Dog. As the kids ran haphazardly through the yard Roxy chased them. I didn't understand at first. The epiphany struck like a major "DUH" moment. Sheep dog, herding errant kids. *I think I put the "less" in "clueless".*

By the time we unpacked ourselves from layers of clothes, gloves wet through and through, boots brimming with snow, fingers were numb and cheeks radiated a rosy glow. All three kids huddled around the pup drying her with fluffy towels they pulled from the linen closet in the hall. Did it matter they were some of my best - and only – high end cotton towels? Catching myself I smiled watching the attentiveness to the newest family member. When the dog emerged from the huddle she seemed happy for all the love and attention.

Hot cocoa with marshmallows and cookies topped off the afternoon. Grilled cheese and chicken soup would be dinner. I make a mean chicken soup. If you're interested you can find the recipe at the back of the book.

Ralph arrived home an hour early. I can't remember the last time he missed work because of the weather. Male pride and a four-wheel-drive truck made him feel invincible. The highways were probably coated with brine and a heavy layer of testosterone.

The dog scampered to him. I thought I saw a hint of adolescent joy in his face. "Okay, I'll admit I'm wrong sometimes but you can't tell anybody. Wouldn't want to ruin my reputation, right?" He cradled the dog in his beefy hands. The three kids joined and suddenly mom was watching. Hubby looked over at me like he understood my feeling left out. Maybe it was more about finagling the dog into our lives. Placing Roxy on the floor gingerly he stepped out of the way of the tangle of hands and feet dancing around the newest addition.

Taking me in his arms he kissed me softly. "You're a sport for allowing the dog."

"I know. You can show your appreciation later." Mischief twinkled in his eyes. "That's not what I'm talking about; ugh!" He kissed me again; this time with more passion.

"Maybe I'll get lucky tonight," he whispered as he squeezed me.

"Is that all you think about?" I pushed him away.

"Meel, you should know me. There are only two things I think about; the last time we had sex and the next time we're gonna have it." Should I fault him for being honest? I think I already knew what he told me. True we weren't into each other that way like we used to be. Life got in the way. How's that song go about yesterdays don't count anymore. I don't believe it. Yesterdays pave the way for tomorrows. Maybe we're not as attractive as we once were. That's okay with me. Physical attraction is only once slice of the marriage pie. Nothing I can do about it anyway. Let's get on with the story.

Pass the Butter

Training the Pooch

    A month later the kids were still fighting over who would walk Roxy. Weather broke from bitter cold; the snow had receded enough to start showing a little bit of the ground, and we could let her run a bit. They taught her how to climb stairs but she was still having a difficult time coming down. When she'd climb the stairs and wanted to come down she would bark and one of the kids would carry her down. Roxy got bigger but was still less than ten pounds. Her little bark, which wasn't constant like some breeds, seemed to speak to us. No matter how much the kids tried to encourage her to trundle down the stairs, she stood at the brink of the stairs unsure of herself.

    Suzanne broke her of the stair phobia by setting up pillows at the base of the sofa and coaxing her, with treats, to climb. Coming down the stairs was a lingering problem because she was built low to the ground. Roxy would go nuts when we opened the front door. There goes that separation anxiety again. After the pup climbed the stairs and looked down helplessly, Suzanne opened the front door. Roxy came storming down the stairs like she was responding to an alarm. That ended another lesson. The kids figured out how to help Roxy get over her challenge. I hoped they remembered to use that cunning in life.

    Next was jumping lessons. The kids wanted her to lay on the sofa with them. At first, they would lift her onto the sofa. She was content until one of them got up, leaving her alone at the top of mount sofa. They seemed oblivious to her plight until one day they initiated couch climbing lessons led by Lisa. Pillows staged to look like a landing zone were set in front of the sofa. Randy would sit on the floor and call her. She struggled at first but when she jumped and landed softly on the pillows, the kids made a big deal over her. I swear there was something magical about Roxy. Even I wanted a part of her. She sat on my lap and I stroked her soft coat. She was gentle. I was beginning to understand why Ralph liked this breed.

By the time she was six months, she was pretty much fully grown. Quirks surfaced; nothing bad just memorable. One was her reaction to the doorbell. When she heard the bell she'd spaz out running to the door and barking then running to the room we where we were sitting. It was like she was trying to tell us someone was at the door. But it didn't end there. She'd run back to the door as if the bark a message to the visitor that she had alerted us to their presence. This happened every time the bell chimed.

Racing to the front door she peered through the one of the dual sidelights.

Wait there, I'll get somebody to open the door.

She'd wait a second to see if the visitor acknowledged her before she scampered to us.

Hey, there's somebody at the door. You need to come see.

She'd run back to the door, glancing back to see if we were following.

I told them you were here. Somebody's coming, I know it.

The other thing causing her to spaz was if one of us went out. She freaked if we didn't take her. When the door opened she charged towards the foyer barking and growling. Inevitably she's hit the area rug in the hall, slam on the brakes and her and the carpet would crash into the front door. You think she'd learn her lesson after a few bumps. This went on for several weeks until my husband thought it was time for a little lesson. Ralph fooled her once when he opened the door and closed it. She came charging out of the Family Room barking, only to be stopped in her tracks when she saw him standing before her. He laughed as she skulked off embarrassed. If you think that deterred her, think again. She's female; we're rarely deterred. I think she laid off the anxiety for a day.

She was good about lots of things. I loved how she kept company when I was home alone; she'd find a comfortable spot on the sofa laying her head on one of the throw pillows. You could almost see the dreamy look in her eyes. Okay, she had me hooked. I loved that little dog more than I thought I could have feelings for anyone other than human family.

Long hair dogs need tender loving care. Roxy's beautiful coat would knot if we didn't brush her regularly. That meant she got the royal treatment every night. The kids shared those responsibilities. Again, Ralph was right about the kids. If I knew it was going to be this easy I wouldn't have been such a naysayer. Roxy did shed and brushing kept it to a minimum; although there were fur deposits on the front-facing surfaces of sofa and loveseat. The kids gave her a monthly bath in the second-floor hall bath. After the first couple of baths she learned to tolerate it. Once she was pretty dry she'd run around proud of her patience knowing a biscuit was her reward. She would rub against any fabric surface at her level, which was between six and eighteen inches high. She was funny like that. She'd rub against the sofa back and forth. Then run around the family room until the dog biscuit came. The first time I vacuumed the sofa I discovered about half a dog worth of fur had clung to the front face of the sofa. I was glad I didn't buy dark furniture. After that revelation I vacuumed everywhere Roxy roamed keeping the colonies of fur bunnies to a minimum.

The toughest times were walking her in the rain. We never seemed to be able to trim her coat enough to keep it from getting dirty. Dry, she looked like a plump ball of fur. When she was bathed or soaked during a walk the weight of water on her coat showed she was really a skinny little thing. We had a collection of towels to dry her. More patience on her part. I wasn't as patient with my hair. Could it be the dog had more patience than me?

One thing I refused to do was to clip her nails. I couldn't watch. Ralph called me a chicken. Roxy didn't like it much and I felt for the poor girl. *Her* nails were being trimmed and *I* needed a drink afterwards. I gave her a treat to tell her I appreciated her being good about the whole thing. She carried the treat to the middle of the family room and worked it over until she had consumed it. I watched her as if every time was the first time. Trimming nails was traumatic and expensive. Our dog's patience saved us from paying the vet or taking her to one of those mammoth pet stores. Didn't like what their pet care department looked like.

"She fascinates you, doesn't she?"

"Got a problem with that buddy?" I turned and smiled. Ralph hugged me. Roxy looked up catching us. I swear it looked like she was smiling; content. I enjoyed watching her gnaw on the biscuit. She surprised me by respecting the furniture and our shoes. She didn't chew on anything unless it was one of her toys. If she did, I hadn't found any evidence.

Pass the Butter

Herding Neurotic Family

    We get the extended family together once a year – most of them lived in southern New Jersey. Somebody has to make the effort. When Ralph's father died, we met cousins from his father's side at the viewing. The luncheon after the funeral attracted faces we hadn't seen in ages. His mother explained there had been a big blow up between Ralph's father and his cousins. According to Dolores, her husband and his cousin Tommy fought over something she considered stupid but kept her opinion to herself after he shut her down. I think it was the only time Ralph' father stood up to Dolores.
    Tommy lived in New Jersey and along with his sister ran a big farm. Apparently all the Ciraccos got together in New Jersey after harvest. The family was generous. There was plenty left on the trees and bushes too ripe to pack and ship but not too ripe to pick and eat. Ralph remembered, painfully, how his father took offense when his cousin offered a selection of fresh fruits and vegetables. When he refused, Tommy tried to reason with him. That made matters worse. Dolores recalled her husband grabbing her and the kids and storming out. She said she tried to reason with him but he was in no mood to talk. She said he carried the grudge like a slap in the face. Regardless, the cousins came to make peace and agreed to visit with us from time to time.
    That blow up was thirty-five years almost to the day he died. My mother-in-law carried the pain of familial rift. She was

influential but not enough to force reconciliation. We didn't realize how much hurt she carried until the funeral and luncheon. Dolores showed emotion I didn't think she possessed. Tears streamed down her cheeks and apologies flowed like a swollen river. My father-in-law's death served a purpose; the family could unite again.

When we met Tommy, now a victim of life's wear and tear on a farmer's body, we saw resemblance between him and his now-departed cousin. No mistaking how the two of them could hold grudges for a lifetime. We were told Tommy mellowed. If this was mellow, he must have been a terror. I saw glimpses of his temper when one of his nephews didn't follow his direction. They had taken on the farm when Tommy and his sister decided to retire. Tommy still felt like nothing could be done correctly without his guidance. His nephews had designs on automating the farm, much to their uncle's chagrin.

Something in the Ciracco family lineage told me grudges and inability to forgive and heal was hereditary. I also realized there was foolish pride that kept the older ones from letting the younger ones lead. I remember thinking, *Is my husband like that too?* I hadn't seen signs. Maybe stubbornness skipped a generation.

Dolores introduced me and reintroduced her son to the Garden State relatives. The same woman whose hard exterior made me avoid her whenever possible, changed that day. Mortality and separation anxiety have a way of bringing pain and in some instances, healing. After watching the power of reunion, Ralph and I decided we would host our extended family once a year to keep the connection. It would also give Dolores support as she adjusted to life as a widow.

Our first big family get together happened in August of the year my father-in-law died. We opened our modest home to all the relatives. People appeared who hadn't attended the March funeral. Final count was sixty-five people. We didn't think the house could handle it but we got through and enjoyed. Our kids met cousins, older cousins sat around and shared homemade wine, fresh produce left over from the harvest and dishes prepared with love and shared liberally. Typical Italian get together, everyone who brought something made enough to feed an army! I made everyone take food home. There was no way we were going to be able to eat all the leftovers. We would have needed an industrial-size refrigerator and freezer to keep things from spoiling.

Roxy was a hit with everyone, even the sect who preferred cats. Her instinct was to create order in what she saw as a herd of people not moving in an orderly manner. Watching her corral people made us laugh. She had her work cut out for her. People milling around, children scampering and frolicking. The little dog wanted to be included. I guess animals have a persona just like people.

Finally the kids attracted her attention tossing a ball and then a Frisbee. The dog played along like one of the kids. Roxy took more walks, everyone wanted to walk her, in one day than she took in a week. By the time the last guest left, we crashed. Like the rest of us, she was exhausted, curling up on the sofa in the Family Room while we picked up after the party.

With all the perishables gone or stored in the fridge, we left the rest of the cleanup for the morning, too tired for anything other than talking. Ralph was happy about how the party came off. We agreed to continue the new tradition. Except for Tommy, who left early, everyone hung around all day. I was trying to figure if he had a problem with crowds, needed alone time or had an anti-social streak. Maybe a combination. He didn't drive; his eyesight was failing. That meant his daughter had to leave with him. His wife, Irish and unaccepted by Tommy's family for the first twenty years of marriage because she wasn't Italian, stayed with us and hopped a ride with a cousin who lived close by.

Wonders never cease to amaze. I thought my family was screwy. Ralph's family was an entire hardware store. We laughed about all the quirkiness. "This better not be you later in life. I don't have the energy to deal with all the horse shit."

"I'll always be my warm wonderful self."

"You call this warm and wonderful? I didn't see your picture next to either word in the dictionary. What spelling did you use?" He flashed a sad face before he hugged and tickled me. I'm so ticklish that threatening to tickle me makes me giggle. The attempt at foreplay fizzled out as we fell asleep in each other's arms. I didn't mind. It wasn't about the sex as much as it was about the emotional connection.

Sunday morning we slept in. There would be cold cereal for breakfast. I didn't have the energy to cook. The kids didn't mind. They slept in as well. In the dining room we ate and talked about the party. We enjoyed hearing the joy and wonder in the questions and conclusions all three of them had drawn. Roxy went out and did her thing in the yard. We could trust her to be outside without a fence or a leash. She knew a good thing.

"Daddy, why are all the boys named Freddy or Sammy?" Suzanne asked. We looked at each other. I hadn't picked up on it. Recalling several times when one of the cousins called Freddy or Sammy, it seemed like half of the guys responded. There was a 'Michael' in the group. His father Freddy was still getting crap from the family for not sticking to the naming convention. It didn't matter that Michael was fifteen at the time of the party. The Ciracco family had a longer memory than most elephants and never let you forget.

Sports and Chauffeurs

Sports took us from the house most weekends. We enjoyed being away from the homestead to watch our children learning to work together to accomplish goals and put their coach's training into action. Kids evolve at their pace. Girls and boys respond to competition differently.

The girls played soccer. They were competitive in a collaborative way. They chased the ball, moving as a group without regard to positioning. That changed as they became more adept at the sport. One of the fascinating things about girls is if there was an injury on the field, play stopped and everyone gathered to comfort the fallen player. It didn't matter whether teammate or foe. I found it refreshing while hubby didn't understand it. This changed as they got older but in the formative years I enjoyed how supportive the girls were towards each other.

Randy tried baseball. His first attempt at bats and balls was this thing they call tee-ball. It's really golf using a bigger ball and a bat instead of a golf club. At first, kids missed the ball as often as they hit it. Ralph would murmur 'mulligan' each time the ball was missed. He called it a whiff. Randy didn't seem to 'get' the whole competitive thing. Hitting a soft baseball off a rubber tee was about as exciting to him as a visit to the pediatrician. The boys were awkward. Fathers yelled for them to run when the ball was struck. The guy standing down the first base line waved to child to run towards him. The children in the field chased the ball and threw it wherever they thought best, was controlled chaos. I was amused by how the fathers reacted, as if every play would decide their child's potential for a major-league contract.

Most boys were uncoordinated; swinging bats too long and heavy at a stationary object on a plastic and rubber tee. When the kids couldn't hit the ball a parent would jump up and help their child. It seemed like the kids didn't care and the parents made too much of their child driving a ball over the heads of outfielders busy watching bees landing on dandelions. Competitiveness that started at an early age was grooming kids for therapy. Some parents were sympathetic, enjoying being around other parents. The ones scaring me, and their children, were those yelling for their kid to hit the ball or make the play. These were the same parents who insisted every kid got a trophy, regardless of winning or losing. There was something to behold; setting kids up for failure. Talk about not learning to cope with minor failures. I was having visions of sore losers and stunned silence when these spoiled children were struck by the hard side of reality.

The girls played collaborative soccer; groups of girls moving like schools of fish chasing the soccer ball around. Arms and legs tangled. A girl fell and the others gathered around to comfort the fallen player. Six-year-old girls cared more about the human side of sports. When they blossomed into teens things got testy. Teenage girls got very competitive. I remember Ralph watching Suzanne play softball. He called it a cat fight. The umpire made a call – who was ever happy with an umpire's call – and sent three girls into a murderous rage. Coaches pulled girls away from a melee as parents shouted things I won't repeat. That was the first and last time Ralph accompanied me to a game.

Pass the Butter

I'm not one to shy away from anything but I refused to be part of educating kids how to be ugly. Three mothers sat at the top of the bleachers down the first base line. We were far enough away we wouldn't get sucked into the yelling and screaming.

At age ten Suzanne wanted to play softball. That survived until she was twelve. After that she gave up on sports; finding the debating club more her speed. When she got really good at debating, we discovered how tough she was. On more than one occasion there were arguments over things she wanted. Her logic was almost flawless. We weren't sure whether to be grateful or frustrated over her persistence. We began to think maybe softball was better for us; all the arguments took place on the field. After games the girls gathered for water ice or ice cream like nothing ever happened. I couldn't say the same for verbal spats over wants and desires.

Playing team sports might be good for developing social skills. Kids had to learn to play together. After the first couple of games and seeing Randy's less than enthusiastic response, I left baseball to my husband. I liked soccer not so much for the type of sport but for the way the kids and parents acted. At least in the early years, soccer was as much social activity as sport. Parents brought lawn chairs, coolers and conversation. I met some great people and also got to see the ugly side of a few of them. I understood how living vicariously through your child could be self-gratifying for the parent but destructive for the child. There were a few instances of parents upbraiding the coach. Other times when parental reaction to a child's honest mistake became a crusade of embarrassment, I began to dislike competitive sports.

Nikki DiCaro

Play Acting

    Lisa used drama to get her way. After a year of soccer she wanted to try dance. She was the one with the audience appeal; never a dull moment when Lisa performed. The latest step performed wherever an audience; she interrupted TV time by putting on an exhibition for us. Suzanne usually went to her room. Randy watched with rapt attention; I think he wanted to join her but was shy. She had enough self-confidence for both of them. She was no Shirley Temple but I don't think Shirley Temple was Shirley Temple.
    Two years into dance, Lisa decided she wanted to act. Dancing wasn't giving her enough attention; at least that how we interpreted it.
    "Everything you do is acting." Her father's statement didn't register.
    "Why do you want to act?"
    She shrugged. "I think it's something I'll like," she said with a flourish and a dance step. Lisa produced a colorful flyer announcing auditions for the school play. We looked at the flyer then at each other.
    "If she wants to act, let's give her the chance." Our middle daughter's face lit up and she ran to her father's arms.
    "Thank you, daddy!"
    "Thank you mother too." I got a big hug and kiss. She knew how to pour it on. Ralph knew I'd be the one to take her to practices and work with her on lines, assuming she got a speaking part so he didn't want to hog all the glory.
    Auditions finally arrived. Lisa was wound tighter than a watch spring. She had us on pins and needles as she spent countless hours practicing lines and asking for feedback. If we

were critical – trying to prepare her for the realities or stage life – we could feel the air get sucked out of the room. This had the potential for being something good or something bad. When Lisa was up, good flowed like honey on a warm day. We tried to temper her enthusiasm; failure would be like nuclear winter.

"Honey, you can get better if you listen to us and work on the parts that could be stronger." We spoke like true wannabes. Ralph was the diplomat. I thought of calling him Kissinger. Lisa listened out of obligation. Puppy dog eyes signaled a cloudburst. Her father hugged her. I thought it was the perfect nonverbal response to our input. If there was a mega-dramatic part in the play I thought she'd get it hands down.

Lisa was awarded a supporting role in the modern version of Romeo and Juliet. When she didn't get the part of Juliet she made peace with her lesser role. "I don't like Jasper anyway." Jasper was the boy who was awarded the part of Romeo. I smiled at her logic. As long as she was happy there'd be peace and harmony at home. For six weeks we lived in virtual R&J reality. That's what Suzanne called it. At first, she played along but she tired quickly. Our oldest had the same level of patience as me; a quart low and slowly dropping.

The weekend of the play finally arrived and not a day too soon. Part of our alternate reality was unconsciously dropping a few of Lisa's lines into conversation. It was funny how much influence our middle child had on the household. She would definitely be an actress on the stage of her life. We wondered if there would be room on her stage for anyone else as she got older. We wouldn't have long to find out.

The play came off well. Lisa was flawless; many admiring parents told her so. The bouquet of flowers we gave her lived in her room until the last petal fell from the solitary rose that survived almost two weeks. We were happy for her accomplishment and hoped she had gotten the acting bug out of her system. There probably would come a time when we wished it hadn't departed so quickly.

Lisa continued to recite lines and playact for us. If there was a scene in a movie we were watching that she liked, she'd get up in front of the television and emulate it. We watched silently, wishing for a commercial interruption. After what seemed like an eternity, Randy walked over to her and quietly took her by the hand and led her to the sofa.

"Can't you see we're trying to watch this movie?" We looked from one child to the other and then at each other. Ralph shrugged. I smiled. Our youngest exercised control over a challenging situation; one where neither of the adults was willing to intercede. This was a glimpse into the quiet confidence of our son, which we learned would serve him well.

Tired of sitting still, Lisa decided to go to Suzanne's bedroom to hang out with her. That was Randy's cue to park his little body between us. He allowed me to hug him for a moment. He was loving but wasn't into my doting. He definitely didn't fit the mold of the youngest child needing reassurance.

Ralph scooped him up and swung him around eliciting giggles and squeals of delight. Then he placed him on the floor on his back and played 'washboard' on Randy's belly. His little body flailed as he giggled uncontrollably. A biology accident was on the horizon if daddy continued. Lisa heard the commotion and stormed into the family room climbing on Ralph's back. That was the cue to play bucking bronco. Both of the young ones would take turns on daddy's back while he crawled around and tried to buck like a wild horse. Lisa wrapped arms around her dad's neck, which shortened the ride as the man-horse wasn't able to breathe. No matter how many times we warned her to hold his shirt collar, she insisted on administering a choke hold.

After a short break in the action the rodeo continued with cowboy Randy up next. He got a longer ride because he was lighter and wasn't choking his father. Lisa made sure we knew she was monitoring the time and announced she would take another ride to ensure she got equal time. She could be brutal when it came to the scales of justice in Lisa's court.

After three rounds of handicapped bronco riding the horse was winded. I was surprised he was able to hold up. He wasn't getting any younger and I reminded him his back wasn't what it used to be. He smiled.

"How about a back rub?" My hands weren't up to it; his back muscles, even as out of shape as he was, were tight and hard. My palms and fingers ached after five minutes of therapy. After that I invested in an electric massager. The gadget looked like E.T. from the neck up. I didn't care if it looked like a zombie. I used that on him, making it much easier on my upper body.

The horseback ride energized the kids. They were playing one of their little games that involved running around the house trying to get away from one another. That lasted all of five minutes and they were back in the family room loud and ornery. Randy jumped onto my lap while Lisa bear hugged my neck. I was bundled in children when Ralph joined. I was barefoot and he took that as open season on my toes; brushing them with his rough hands. I didn't like to be tickled and he knew it. If you want to see a Tasmanian devil in action, just attempt to tickle me. I kicked and flailed. Ralph knew better than to get close.

The kids were minor casualties of the guerilla assault; ending up on either side of me sprawled on the sofa.

"Oh no! Mommy's sorry!" I felt bad; shooting the evil eye at the culprit before hugging both kids. Ralph rose heavily. His knees popped and complained.

"Serves you right for tickling me." He winked before turning towards to kitchen for what he called a well-deserved beer. I followed him; the kids in tow. It was ice cream time. Each of the kids had their favorite bar. I stopped buying tubs of decadent pleasure after Randy was born. I had no self-control when it came to sweets. I could devour an entire quart in one sitting. Switching to controlled portions helped me contain the urge to binge. Suzanne wasn't much into sweets. She was conscious of her diet even when she was pre-teen. I could have learned from her but my willpower was low after fighting the good parent / provider fight every day. I found comfort in food; much to the detriment of my wardrobe.

Pass the Butter

The Two Point Slow

We weren't wealthy, by any means. We endeavored to be good stewards of what wealth we earned. We also felt strongly about ensuring our kids understood the value of a dollar. Sure, we were frivolous sometimes. Show me someone who wasn't frivolous at least once in their life and I'll show you a Franciscan Monk.

All three kids made it through college with minimal loans. We agreed to match whatever scholarship money they were awarded. That dollar for dollar match meant something even to our late stage teenagers. We were able to fund most of the uncovered tuition; with the kids contributing towards room and board, books and activity fees. They were required to work to earn part of their future. It was a good way to build accountability and responsibility.

One area we felt required our support was automobiles. "They can't work if they can't get to the job. I'm sure neither one of us will feel like driving to and picking up." Ralph's logic was, well, logical. He and I wanted them in sturdy cars that didn't have rocket engines and weren't sexy. We thought sexy translated into joy rides and too many friends piled in for field trips.

Suzanne was the first car shopper. She was picky; she called it discerning. We looked at used cars that were fairly large. Our oldest called them gas guzzlers; convincing us the savings on vehicle cost was going to be consumed by the cost of fuel and repairs. Her sights were set on a Volkswagen Rabbit. She and her father called around to dealers. The car she wanted was popular and hard to find. In the end she settled for the 2.0-liter engine. The 1.8-liter turbo was going to take too long and she needed a car for college.

Three weeks after the dealer took our order he called announcing the car was being shipped to their location. The four-door with hatch back was cute and a little too small for my taste. I knew it was either that model or complicated commuting and possibly no employment so we settled.

The car passed Ralph's initial tests. One of his friends was a mechanic and agreed to put the car on the lift and take her through diagnostic testing. The prognosis was good so we closed the deal. At first Suzanne was enthralled. I think part of the excitement was winning the model discussion. She was never one to back down or celebrate compromise or defeat. This was important to her; important enough to give her some room.

By month four the car had become an extension of her. After freshman year the bloom was off the rose. She was home for the summer and working full-time at a local retailer. One night we were gathered around the dinner table; that rare occasion when all the kids were in the house together. Conversation swirled around high school and college. Suzanne was flaunting her knowledge and watching her siblings hang on her words. That didn't last long. Conversation was turning towards Lisa's vehicular aspirations. It was her turn for wheels.

"Suze, Dad's taking me out to look at cars. Do you really like yours? I think it's cute."

"It works for me." Randy was watching the volley between his sisters.

"Would you be upset if I got one too?" Lisa was the pleaser and looked up to her big sister.

"Get whatever you want. I don't think there's any law against sisters having the same car. You might want to get a different color."

"Uh, yeah!"

"And get the turbo. You won't be happy with the two point slow." Randy decided to join the conversation by tossing a verbal grenade into the discussion.

"Why do you have to be such an asshole?" Suzanne's delivery was shrill.

"Hey, none of that language in this house," I said sternly. Ralph played silent spectator.

"It's true; you even said it!" Randy continued to poke his sister. Color rose in her neck. I'd seen that look and it was a signal to change the subject.

"I like Suzanne's car. Speed doesn't matter, right dad?" Lisa asked.

"That's right." He didn't sound convincing.

"Besides, insurance costs more for faster cars and they consume more gas. More insurance and more gas means less spending money." My logic sounded flawless. Unfortunately it didn't align with teen logic.

"When it's my turn to get a car, I'm getting something sporty," Randy announced proudly. My husband and I exchanged looks. He was our dreamer.

"I don't care, I love Suzanne's car and I want one just like it!" Lisa rose with a flourish and hugged her sister. The only thing missing was the honeycombs and the bees. The conversation broke down from there signaling clean up time. I cooked so the kids washed and dried. Sitting in the family room, my feet on the ottoman and paperback novel on my lap, I considered the interchange over cars. Things we took for granted were new and frightening experiences for kids although their façade of bravado magnified how much they had to learn about life.

I tried not to laugh at Randy's two point slow comment. The kid's wide-eyed wonder and almost nonexistent filter made for interesting repartee. I could have said 'conversation' but 'repartee' sounded sophisticated, right? I could mangle other languages with the best of them!

Hubby joined me and powered up the boob tube. Funny word 'boob'. It carried negative connotations yet men were captivated by large ones and dismissive of small ones. The same thing went for breasts. He harrumphed through several channels. The older he got the stranger the sounds his body made. I got over the farting and burping long ago. I was convinced there was a gene deficiency in men that made them marvel over oral and rectal emissions. Ralph could leave a vapor trail a mile long when he ate the wrong foods. I tried in vain to modify his diet; never intimating it had *anything* to do with the sounds and smells.

"What did you make of the car discussion?" I didn't have to look at the television to know there was a commercial break.

"I don't know. I think it's a kid thing and they'll grow out of it before I ever hoped to gain an understanding of their logic."

"Hhmm." He was processing. I think he wanted a less cerebral answer. I wasn't in that mood; still trying to digest where the babies had gone.

"Exactly." Before the conversation could lift off, his show was back. I reverted to the love story I read without absorbing. My babies were growing up too fast and I felt like I was falling further and further behind the curve of understanding them. Was I like them when I was their age? *Of course you were. Do you really think you were special?* The voice of reason decided to add her twenty-five cents – inflation made two cents less valuable.

"I think it's good they're at least sharing their opinions."

"Talking to the television?"

"No, I was talking to you."

"Is that a commercial?" I couldn't help myself. He shot a look overflowing with disdain.

"Do you think it's good they're sharing?" he asked.

"If I could connect with the logic I'd feel so much better." The nagging itch of uncertainty made it impossible to scratch it away.

"Look, they're together and they're not fighting."

"We raised them right."

"Are you feeling okay? You sound like something's bothering you." He knew me too well.

"I'm fine."

"Meel, talk to me."

"What?" I hoped my one-word deflections would stop the alien probe from entering my cerebral cortex.

"You only read beach novels when you need to escape. You don't need to escape me."

"Now look what you did," I said. The words felt like frozen molasses in my throat. He encouraged me out of the chair and pulled me into him.

"I love you for being so soft and caring." Tears spilled from me as I buried my face in his shoulder. He held me for a long time. I broke from his embrace and walked across the room; stopping in front of the television.

"I didn't ask for this." He sported a puzzled look.

"Ask for what?"

"For my kids, our kids, to grow up." I hugged myself trying to regain composure. He smiled wanly.

"You think I like getting older?" I shook my head. "Look at how successful they are. Suzanne's doing well in college. Lisa's getting ready to graduate and Randy's a typical last child with all the energy we once had."

"Did we have that much energy? It seems like so long ago that I don't remember." I was becoming Princess of the land of Feel Sorry for Yourself. I don't know why he put up with me. I cut him off before he could respond. "I'm having a down hormone day. Seems like I have them often. I don't like feeling this way but I have to let it out or I'll go nuts." My stare told him to forget about saying something sarcastic.

"I'm happy you're thinking like that."

"I know you've been patient."

"No more patient than you've been with my insisting on fixing things that should have gone in the trash." I almost fell over. I thought he was oblivious to my comments. "I do those things because it brings back memories of my father teaching me. Dad wasn't perfect but nobody is. He taught my brother and me valuable lessons. One of them was to choose a mate who would make us better persons. You've done that for me."

"You're trying to make me cry again, aren't you?"

"I'm telling you this because you're a wonderful wife and amazing mom. You are a big part of why our three can be in the same room for more than five minutes and not start a riot."

"Thank you. I needed to hear that encouragement. Sometimes I get so wrapped up in life I forget to take time to enjoy our accomplishments."

"That's why I'm here to remind you. It's in the job description of the husband. To love, cherish and remind. That was in our vows, if I remember correctly." I smiled and rushed to his arms. We kissed passionately. I heard noise from the dining room. I turned to see the three of them watching us.

"How long have you three been standing there?"

"Long enough to experience your PDA," Suzanne said. They stood in unison for another minute before disbursing. I blushed.

"What's PDA?" He asked.

"Public Display of Affection. At least I think that's right." For good measure he kissed me again.

I gently pushed back from him. "Okay Romeo, time to break it up. Bad enough the kids caught us."

"They're old enough. Let's have an adult play date," he said.

"Not while they're up. Remember the first time you imagined your parents getting intimate?" His expression turned serious.

"Oh yeah. It felt unnatural."

"Exactly. How do you think they'd perceive our disappearance?"

"I don't think they'd believe it was aliens."

"If we sneak off and have sex while they've up and around, they're gonna think we're aliens!" We both laughed at my attempt to be funny before settling onto the sofa. The house was eerily quiet after the kids retreated to their bedrooms to catch up on homework. Was this an indication of empty nesting? I dismissed the thought before melancholy swept over me like a rogue wave.

Nikki DiCaro

Baby on Board

I don't understand the need to hang a placard on the car that announces a child is a passenger. Is this quasi-royalty gone wrong? We've seen plenty of these signs. Have you wondered the purpose? First and foremost for me is pride. People want to know they are with child; like it's some huge accomplishment to have a child. I have three and I'm not announcing it to the world. Is this supposed to inform other drivers to give wide berth or to pay no heed to erratic driving? It could be positive but I think it's got the potential to carry significant risk. Kidnappers would be fully informed if they were looking to snatch a baby. I'll bet placard purchasers never considered that exposure point.

Is it to inform emergency crews in case of an accident? I could see it now, God forbid there's a serious accident. Emergency service teams arrive and begin the task of extracting vehicle occupants.

"Wait Joe, what're you doing?"

"What's it look like, Fred? I'm going to pry open the doors and get everyone out that's trapped."

"Did you do a walk around the vehicle to see if there were any placards telling us who's inside."

"But the vehicle's upside down."

"Doesn't matter. People pay good money to hang those signs on their vehicles. We have to make sure they get their money's worth."

"You're not serious."

"Like a heart attack."

"Speaking of a heart attack, I think the driver is convulsing."

"You go ahead and check for signage and I'll keep the gawkers back."

What if you have twins, triplets or more? Do you hang one sign for each child or do you have a sign that reads 'babies' plural? Maybe if we really believe the placards mean something important we could hang other information signs. I like the idea of 'husband on board'. This way if we appear lost, people will understand it's because we won't stop to ask directions.

What about 'multi-tasker on board'. This way when you see a vehicle swaying, changing lanes without warning or driving slow in the passing lane we can surmise that person's texting, eating or applying eye liner.

I like 'self-centered egotist on board' and 'poor planner on board'. These two ditties inform why you're being tailgated, cut off and generally placed in peril when they're near.

There is a huge market for placards. I think the business potential is enormous and most of the market is untapped. You probably think I'm daft, right? Think again. This nonsense started with bumper stickers. We'll delve into that lunacy next. Let's continue down the rabbit hole of window art.

There are those who insist on placing stick figure outlines for each family member. Why is it important to advertise your family size? And why on a vehicle?

"Wait Fred, there's stick figures on the back window. Looks like husband, wife, three kids and a dog. Better get the inventory sheet."

"Hey Joe, how do you know they're husband and wife; maybe they're cohabitating."

"So what?"

"Habitating. You know, like living together but not with paper."

"Never thought about that. I got a real problem with people living in sin."

"Fred, you're not serious?"

"Remember that heart attack you were having? Well I'm having one of them."

"But you took an oath."

"I can't violate my moral obligations."

Can you see how crazy this could get? Well that's why I think there's money to be made. Thinking about the military, they advertise years of service and rank. Maybe I could invent ways to make similar placards or adhesive signage.

Signs like: first owner, second owner, x number of years of ownership, what you paid for the vehicle (for all those with an inferiority complex who need to try to make themselves superior to others), mileage successes (100,000 miles, etc.). Accident frequency – that would be popular for personal injury lawyers. The opportunities are endless.

Let's segue to bumper stickers. Let's start with the risks of vehicular-borne announcements. Times have changed. Respect for personal property has degraded to the point you might expect slashed tires, bashed headlights or smashed windows if your bumper sticker message inflamed someone with no self-control or nothing to lose. More arguments had exploded into violence than ever before. And people feel justified applying their rage to others. That's one of the reasons I have no signage on my car. I don't even let the car dealers advertise their name on my car. When I bought the Benz I asked the salesperson how much they were going to pay to advertise their dealership on my car. The salesperson cocked his head and looked at me like a plant was growing out of my head.

"Really, you want me to be a mobile billboard for your dealership?"

"Not exactly."

"Then what *exactly* would you call having your name on my car?" The salesperson looked at me like there was a bird building a nest in the plant growing out of my head.

"Our name's on every car," he replied, trying to justify.

"I'll be the exception to that rule. Want me to buy the car, take your name off or let's discuss an advertising fee."

"Let me see what I can do," he said disgusted with me. I drove the car from the dealership with no advertisements. I think the salesperson had concluded there was something wrong with me. There would not have been enough time in the day to explain.

Okay, back to the bumper sticker thing. What do you think of all the 'proud' parents? Proud of their honor student, their athlete, their dancer, musician, etc.

Then there are the counterculture people who spend money for signage that shows how little they have progressed from prepubescence. My personal favorite is 'My dog is smarter than your honor student'. Really? Someone thought that was pithy and appropriate? How would they know? Was their dog Mister Peabody? Could the dog speak and handle complex math problems? I'm not sure that would be possible without opposable thumbs. So many educational materials require the ability to grasp, handle and work calculator, pencil, books, so on and so forth.

Another popular one that shows our penchant for violence is "My kid beat up your honor student". Now that's the zenith of maturity. Encourage your child to bully what he or she can't be. Better yet, show the world how incredibly childish you can be. I steer clear of people who sport signage with that content. You never know when one of them might react badly to something you do while driving.

Other countries make fun of us for being so shallow. We do nothing to dissuade their mockery. We seem to be proud of the criticism. This is the same bunch that will swing first and think later if you look at them cross. I think the whole 'need to tell the world what's on our mind' is amusing. What in the name of all that's holy prompts people to do thoughtless stuff? I'd like to think it's ignorance, but that would be branding a significant portion of our population as ignorant. I refuse to dismiss this silliness to innocence.

Yo Amelia, you're taking the whole judgment thing too far. Keep it up and you'll have a reality television show or be draped in a black robe passing judgment on people who would do or reveal almost anything for their five minutes of fame.

I'm glad I'm beyond the child-bearing years. I don't think I'd have to moxie to raise kids in this brave new world.

One of Ralph's high school buddies, Tony Mario (I know, he has two first names) is a Pennsylvania State Trooper. He looked like he was chiseled from a block of granite. He was a little shorter than my husband but he looked solid. High cut hair; brown on top and gray on the sides. Deep brown eyes set in a ruddy clean-shaven face, bookended an aquiline nose. He had an easy way about him but had that air of authority and control. When he and his wife, Martha, were over for dinner he told an interesting story. He had been following a late model black sedan on Route 352. The car had a few interesting pieces of car art (my vernacular for bumper stickers). One said 'Love Thy Neighbor'. She was tailgating an old car and laying on the horn. When she was finally able to pass them, she flipped them the bird.

Another sticker read 'Slow Down; Enjoy Life'. She ran two yellow lights and almost T-Boned another car. Her license plate, a vanity plate, read 'Patiens' (you can have up to seven characters on the plate). She passed three cars that weren't going fast enough; apparently yelling something choice at them. After that incident, he pulled her over. Approaching the car cautiously he made her exit the vehicle slowly before checking her for weapons. She was livid; barking complaints and expletives. She refused to surrender identification, which made him suspicious. He cuffed her and placed her in the back of his cruiser. Tracking down the vehicle registration and running it through the state's database he was puzzled. Turning to the woman, whose face was beet red he asked, "Is that your car?"

"F*** yes!" She shouted. He shook his head as he sized her up. "Why did you pull me over and cuff me? I don't have any outstanding violations?" He paused before responding.

"I read the bumper stickers and your license plate. The owner was all about peace, love and patience. When I saw you acting like a crazed person trying to escape, I thought the car must have been stolen." He leveled his gaze. She looked sheepishly at him; apology mixed with embarrassment.

"I'm gonna let you off with a warning. The next time you think of doing something stupid, think of what you're telling the world you stand for and try to act like you believe it." He removed the cuffs slowly and returned her vehicle information. She pulled away slowly. He hoped she wouldn't kill herself or someone else.

"I'm not sure if that's sad or funny," I said.

"I stopped trying to figure people. It takes too much energy and always fails me," Martha said.

"I don't envy you, my friend," Ralph said, handing him another long neck.

"It's all part of the job. My satisfaction was scaring the shit out of her," Tony said, smiling. I think he enjoyed the power trip. I'd never fault him. He's in a thankless job and might be asked to put his life on the line at any moment.

Tony's got a morbid streak, the little voice – one of many in my head – announced. Ralph was making a joke about the whole thing. It must be a guy thing. Martha appeared to be unsettled by the story.

Hey sugar, it's not like you're pure or something. Remember that little encounter in the mall parking lot when somebody snatched your parking space? I recall you trying to conjure up a little payback. The voice was enjoying a resurgence. I wanted it to enjoy a silence relapse.

I'm not religious, spiritual yes. I offered silent thanks that my husband had a job that didn't put him in harm's way. Tony's little episode with the crazy driver could have ended differently. We've become less tolerant of law enforcement. Is it the 'law' or the 'enforcement' that's got people intolerant? Shooting police is nutso, off the rails, gonzo, lunacy! We despise until we need them. Same story, different cast of characters. I remember Martha sporting a full head of thick jet black hair. The long luxurious strands broke softly over her shoulders and framed her olive complexion, hazel eyes and thin and slightly upturned nose. Full lips made me wish I could tolerate needles – lip plumping and all. Since all the violence against law enforcement, Martha's hair had begun to display strands of stiff gray hairs. She began to look her age.

We talked about hair color. She tried once but the results weren't worth the effort or the money. I was a do-it-yourself hair color amateur. I offered to help Martha. I'm not sure if she didn't trust me or didn't think it mattered to Tony. I wasn't naïve, I knew it mattered to men.

Pass the Butter

Oblivious to Over - Confidence

Friends tell me stories of children who run from them like they're infected with a deadly virus. Liberated, new and untested freedom in hand, these overconfident children crash through remnants of emotional and moral guardrails their parents erected to provide precious time for them to mature and gain knowledge and discernment. After weeks, months or years, the prodigal return with wounded pride and bruised ego. And parents take them back as relief washes over them like the first seasonal rains over sunbaked ground.

Kids have no frame of reference upon which to base life-altering decisions. They may take advice from friends or from the Internet or both. It's easy to make decisions that aren't based on tested reality. Making the decision and living with the consequences are as polar opposite as fire and ice.

Youth have outsized confidence borne on the wings of bravado. My kids had it. Fortunately, they didn't decide to do anything rash. Our brood knew better. We told them early on they would never have it better than living at home. Their look of disbelief made Ralph laugh until he almost cried. After my motherly threat to disown them if they tried anything stupid, hubby pulled me aside and told me I would have been a big hit during the Spanish inquisition.

I didn't think I was out of line. Better to shut the barn door while the cows were still inside. I knew this overwrought sense of knowledge and experience didn't yield the expected results.

Kids that ran off towards the illusion of unfettered freedom devoid of obligations got rude awakenings. My mother used to say, if you think life's easier if you didn't live here, you're in for a rude awakening. I never understood what a rude awakening was. When I asked what she meant, I think she turned a shade of red I couldn't remember seeing even in the Crayola crayon box.

So, the kids are gone – those ungrateful heathens! Yay, right? El wrongo! Parents fret, worry and agonize over their children's plight and hate themselves for doing a poor job of keeping the birdies in the nest. Unhealthy doses of suffering, enough to go around, plague all with regret and self-doubt. My kids stayed put until college. I worried when they went off to college, tuition pretty much covered and our relationship about as strong as it could have been.

Regardless of the consequences that cause children to run away, all things come to an end, for good or for ill. In the end, the parties reconcile. Sometimes the psychological and physical damage is temporary. Other times it's permanent, as in drug or alcohol addiction or worse. Overdose and death aren't as unusual as in prior eras. Maybe the destruction was equivalent across eras. Maybe because everyone wasn't a news stringer with a video-enabled mobile phone, nothing much has changed except the immediacy and pervasiveness of information and misinformation. Whatever the reason, things can be better or worse, depending upon how you deal. Dealing from the bottom of life's deck will catch up with the gambler eventually. It always does.

"Earth to Amelia." I made an abrupt return from Funk Town.

"What?" I looked at my husband. He was sending facial smoke signals.

"You zoned out." *No, just a little walk down Main Street of Funk Town.*

"I guess I snoozed for a minute." *For all I knew I could have fallen asleep for hours.*

"How many seconds in your minutes?" He smiled. I didn't think it was funny.

"What did you make of Tony and Martha?"

"A married couple." *Welcome, Mister Smart Ass. Won't you join us?*

"That's good. Do you want to risk thirty-two dollars and try for the sixty-four-dollar question?"

"You mean the whole State Trooper thing?" *No, I mean the haircut.* Crinkled lips and wrinkled brow responded. "I think he's nuts to stick around after his twenty." That was the first logical thing he's said.

"Would you retire if you could?" I'm not sure why I needed to ask.

"Sure, if I had a hobby."

"What would you do to keep yourself busy?"

"Get a hobby." *Oh, this was going nowhere at break neck speed.*

"Such as?"

"A hobby, you know?" *If I knew I wouldn't ask.*

"Fixing appliances?" *God forbid.*

"That would be interesting." He was playing coy. That was the beer talking. When he was one pull over the line he thought he was a junior comedian. I could see the driveway overflowing with carcasses of refrigerators, freezers and stoves; my version of Fred Sanford. I liked that show; especially Grady. He had that dry delivery that sprayed sarcasm all over the scenery.

"Don't you need a license to do that?"

"I have one. It has my picture on it."

"What?" I had to process for a beat while I tried to read his complexion. "You're shitting me."

"No, I'm house trained." He winked. "I'd go work for somebody. Could you imagine the garage filled with broken appliances begging to be repaired?" *No, not in this lifetime.*

"Who does that work and would hire you?" That came out wrong. His lips formed a pout. The salt and pepper stubble made the expression feel sad. "I didn't mean for it to sound like that."

"I get it. My job's not that bad. Besides, I like fixing things when I feel like it. If I had to do it for somebody else, it wouldn't be any different that my day job." He had a point.

"Retirement needs to be planned," I said, as if it was some big epiphany.

"You thinking of retiring?" It was a fair question.

"If I could keep from sitting around all day eating and getting old, I'd think about it. But only if we could afford it."

"That's what makes this conversation fun."

"What? Me getting old and fat?"

"Come on Meel; it's just conversation. We couldn't afford for either of us to retire yet. If we really want to dig into this, we can work through a few options." Digging sounded like manual labor. Making plans to retire was like planning a trip to the moon. It might not be possible in my lifetime.

"I don't hate my job," I said defensively.

"That's a big vote of confidence," he replied playfully.

"I don't want to talk about this anymore because we can't do anything about it." He made a Ralph line for the kitchen. "Bring me one of your craft beers." He stopped and stared at me as if I asked him to cook a French dinner. Craft beer; that's like one of those weird phrases that caught on despite of the silliness. Crafts were things you cut out and stapled or glued together. I doubt Ralph's beer had glue as one of its ingredients. Although… Never mind.

Pass the Butter

Routines and Disruptions

The mass transit authority decided to replace large sections of track on my regional rail route. They chose the summer to do it. That meant they would bus commuters around the work zone. The ride was long enough without introducing ore complexity. Did I have a choice? They stopped consulting me before they started major repairs.

I had to find another way to work unless I wanted to play musical vehicles. I could imagine this commuter shuffle running as efficiently as a fire drill in the dark. Driving was an option. You know how entertaining rush hour commuting is for me. I'd get to reconnect with all my distracted friends. I needed to buy a year's supply of patience if I was going to drive. I'd have to warn Ralph too. I think he considered divorcing me the last time I drove to work for an extended period. This construction project was scheduled to take three weeks. I knew SEPTA's major repair timetable was like the half-life of uranium and about as predictable.

"I might be driving to work for a month," I announced over dinner. He stopped the fork between plate and mouth.

"Did you alert Penn DOT? I'm sure they'd want to make accommodations."

"Very funny there Groucho."

"Seriously. Some states have HOV lanes. Penn DOT could set up an AOL."

"What would an old Internet browser company have to do with highways?" I impressed myself that I knew what AOL stood for.

"Amelia Only Lane. Sounds catchy don't you think?"

"Oh, I think you caught something. I hope it's not contagious!" I continued eating while he stared at me. I smiled through a forkful of Sicilian chicken. I don't think he appreciated my one-upping him.

I had another week to decide how I was going to deal with disruption to my routine. The downside was longer commuting time. I could drive to another regional rail line, like Media. That would add time on the front end and back end. Either way, dealing with the commuter shuffle or driving to another line, the commute was probably going to be a half hour longer. Doesn't sound like much, right? That's one hour each day, five hours a week and at least fifteen hours until repairs are finished.

I'm pretty protective of my time. Cutting into sleep or evening was going to make me irritable. My husband would end up getting the short end of that stick. He wasn't into sticks, unless it was butter.

The shuffle day arrived. I decided to try the multi-vehicle exchange to see how painful it would be. I didn't want to battle more driving. I was going to find out how intolerant I really was. I probably didn't need to use mass transit to learn. I could have asked my husband. He was a font of Amelia knowledge.

The ride started out uneventfully. There was an air of adventure. I wish there would have been an air of efficiency and silence. I was a hopeless romantic when it came to routine. People talked like we were going to experience the eighth wonder of the world. The only wonder was whether I was going to get to work when the timetable indicated. That would be major, colonel or even general.

The closer we got to the transfer point – that's the technical term SEPTA used – people got giddy. The last time I got giddy was with the help of champagne. If they were serving alcohol, I couldn't find it. The whole process sounded official and efficient. I thought it sounded hokey. This was the mass transit agency. They used to be called the 'authority'. I think they dropped it when they discovered they had no authority and they were not an authority on the mass movement of commuters.

The strangle point for this commute was leaving the railcars and lining up to board buses. Surface travel by bus during rush hour was going to be painful. Buses weren't the gazelle of surface vehicles. They were more like a cross between snail and caterpillar. My apologies to Earth's indigenous creatures.

I climbed aboard one of the fleet of buses and found a seat for what was scheduled to be a twelve-minute ride. The best laid plans of mice and men were meant to be upended. I discovered I could hide in the music on my mobile phone. It helped a little. The bus environment must have been sprayed with truth serum. People were talking so much and so loud I began to think the off-switch was broken. I never had that much to say. I wished others would have discovered that truth. I did learn things about my newest commuting buddies that were probably best left unsaid. It's amazing what people will share. I value my privacy. Hey, secrets make me feel mysterious; and probably less boring.

This chapter of the morning shuffle lasted twenty minutes. I couldn't get off the truth bus fast enough; almost knocking three people over. "Excuse me, I'm feeling sick." I placed a hand firmly over my mouth to emphasize the oral evacuation process that was about to begin. There were a few sympathetic words and more conclusions about morning sickness, too much spicy food or alcohol. At least people didn't disappoint.

I decided to walk the nine blocks to the office instead of climbing the stairs and riding another train into Center City from 30th Street Station. The weather was slowly migrating to humid but the dew point hadn't climbed high enough to make me need a shower after the walk. I forgot how exhausting walking was. It didn't help that I was wearing three inch chunky heels. Halfway there it was too late to turn back. Thankfully a coffee shop appeared like a mirage. I decided I deserved a reward for being intrepid. A reprimand might have been more appropriate.

This shop didn't have fancy names for their beverages. I wasn't in the mood to learn more urban-speak. Iced coffee with lots of half and half provided the fuel to get me to the office. Checking my phone for the time, I was going to be a few minutes late. T-squared (Tony Testosterone), that's what my colleagues and I decided to settle on. We thought Mister T wasn't appropriate because our boss wasn't into ostentatious jewelry or Mohawk hair. He was beginning to sport a horseshoe Mohawk. You know, hair on three sides and none on top. My father, God rest his soul, used to call that look 'divot head'. My dear dad died with almost a full head of hair.

The five-minute rest and twelve ounces of high octane java lit me up for the rest of the walk. When I got to the office, one of the girls warned me that T-Squared was looking for me. I parked my shoulder bag at my workspace, logged on the computer system and checked email. I knew he would ask if I read his email. He liked to drop an electronic hand grenade in my mailbox just before he called me into his office. I would have been foolish not to learn from history.

I was ready for him. I think that deflated his overblown ego; meaning the meeting was more about my being a few minutes late than missing an important deadline. He liked to impose deadlines when it suited him. I wasn't into suits although my close-knit group of colleagues had thought about a lawsuit to send a message to Mount Olympus that there was trouble in the mythical land where all the work got done.

By lunch I was ready to go home. Grabbing my bag lunch I found a quiet spot in the lunch room and flipped through my phone. I muted the volume to keep the little electronic nuisance quiet until I was ready to let it interrupt my life. I missed a

Pass the Butter

couple of calls so I checked voicemail. One message was from a company that had 'learned I was drowning in student debt and was looking for help to be bailed out.' I hadn't been a student for three decades. When I was in college, tuition wasn't the cost of a four-bedroom house. I'm not sure how they knew I couldn't swim. Drowning was something I feared but I never went swimming in debt lake. Therefore, I didn't need swimming lessons. Oh yeah, on the bail out thing, I wasn't too big to fail. Don't get me wrong, I was larger than I wanted.

Nikki DiCaro

I Meant Well

Some phrases haunt me. Welcome to Amelia's House of Horrors! I meant well is one of those. Andy, also known as Tony Testosterone or T squared, said that to me when Joanie ran to the ladies' room crying.
"I don't know why she's crying."
"Really? You think that was productive? Sure seems like she appreciated you embarrassing her in front of the office." He was fishing for sympathy. The lake had already been drained. He was too dumb to realize.
"I was trying to help her."
"Try razor blades and a warm bath next time."
"Amelia, I don't think you're being fair."
"Oh now we're in blame thrower mode." *Step right up and try your luck. Three balls for a quarter. Throw the blame and if it sticks, you get to pick a stuffed animal for your lady.*
"What? Amelia, sometimes I wonder why leadership thinks your management material." *Because they know you're not.*
"There you go again Mister Sympathetic." He was my boss and I was teaching him the finer points of not cratering the morale.
"I resent that remark."
"If the shoe fits…" The burn in his stare told me daggers were being prepared.
"You know I have forty people to manage."

"You're doing a fine job of managing them down to thirty-nine."

"You think she's gonna quit? Maybe she's not cut out for this job." *I know something I'd like to cut out.*

"You better let Lora know."

"Lora, why?"

"No, Lora Schmidt."

"That's rich." *Not as rich as Joanie could be if she sues.*

"Seriously? Are you dense or did you really think Joanie thought you meant well when you dressed her down?"

"I guess you're right." *The guessing game, one of my favorites.* Can't believe he thinks the job is a game and we're markers to be moved around the board. The only thing that fits his game scheme is that coming to work every day is a game of chance like rolling the dice. You might find him in a good mood - rolling a seven – or find him vile or surly – rolling snake eyes.

"You're being sarcastic." *Of course I am; you would know. You really do think you meant well. You were probably alone in that conclusion. You had to explain. Does that tell you something? Come here, let me help get that common sense to the front of the file cabinet that's your brain.* Yikes, that sounded eerily like my mother.

Meaning well is cousin to 'I mean you know'. Ever heard that phrase? My sister used it so much I began to call her the 'you know' girl.

"Amelia, I mean, you know!"

"No, I don't know. Please tell me."

"Why don't you tell me?" She replied, starting the adolescent back and forth of trivial bantering.

"How much time do you have? You know I can give you lots of reasons."

"You're being childish." Another of my sister's dismissive phrases. She could call me childish because she was the foremost authority on the subject.

"You should know."

"What's that supposed to mean?"

"There's no hidden meaning. This isn't a Cracker Jack box or Captain Crunch cereal box. There's nothing hidden." At the ripe age of thirteen I was honing my sarcasm to a razor's edge. She would cross her arms tightly across her smallish chest, stamp her left foot several times before storming off to report me to the warden, my mother the wielder of the wooden spoon.

"I'm telling mom!" She exclaimed, her words trailing off. I had a few minutes before Mother Nature unleashed parental fury on me. The wooden spoon was more threat than reality. If I was foolish enough to be within striking distance I might catch the tail end of a swat. Sister dear would listen for telltale signs of the argument; hoping mon would put me in my place. The first few times I refused to yield. That was a serious miscalculation. Mom always had the right-of-way when she was scolding. Once I learned to shut my trap and open my ears, mom because more compassionate. That meant Category 1 rather than Category 5 wind strength.

No long after I grew bigger ears, my sister realized her ratting me out was going to amount to nothing more than her incessant complaining. I think my mother tired of it and went through the motions. Eventually I stopped acting like a spoiled brat and my sister stopped engaging in frivolous arguments. Even mom was surprised by my sister's rapid maturity. I think she knew I was a hopeless case. More than once she warned me not to give others a reason to dislike me. I didn't have the heart to tell her I was a lawyer in my former life.

"I pity the poor man who marries you." *Don't worry mom, I'm not planning on marrying a poor man.* I tried to appear contrite. She offered a wan smile laced with resignation. I think she had several private conversations with Ralph when she realized things were getting serious between us. It wasn't until we were married that he disclosed the veiled warnings about me.

Pass the Butter

"Your mother had no idea I was looking for a strong woman." He hugged me. "Never change," he said forcefully. I don't think he knew what he was asking. I didn't plan to change and I don't think he truly understood the depth and breadth of the sarcastic and independent streak that raced like jagged bolts of lightning through me.

Nikki DiCaro

Unconscious! Bias!

Society is finally awakening to the fact that we're riddled with unconscious bias. Maybe 'riddled' isn't the appropriate word. That term brings back memories of the old Batman television show with Adam West and Burt Ward and Frank Gorshen as The Riddler. Riddled has come to mean the past tense of puzzle or conundrum or brain teaser. In the Prohibition Era, riddled meant to be shot full or holes or filled with lead. Maybe it's better to say 'filled with unconscious bias'.

If you think like me, God help you, you're wondering if there is both conscious and unconscious bias. This is one of the few times the answer is yes! I'm not here to explain the differences and similarities. I'm here to ask snarky questions regarding both 'unconscious' and 'bias'. Unconscious relates to lack of consciousness or lack of awareness. You're unconscious when you get knocked out or asleep. There are other less flattering ways to describe unconscious. I'll leave that to your imagination.

Am I the only person who thinks people sleepwalk through life? Look around and take notice. What? You don't study people? I understand. Studying was difficult enough in school, with the nun hovering over us with yardstick in hand and scowl on her face. I think many people seem awake but they're numb or unconscious. Doubt me, doubt my wisdom. See for yourself… or see for someone else if you have multiple personalities.

Pass the Butter

I'm unconscious sometimes. My husband will attest to that. I'll admit it rather than be dragged before the court of public opinion and berated for perjuring myself. I'd love to perjure someone else but I don't think that's possible without being a ventriloquist. There are drugs that can cause you to do things when you're unconscious. Reports of people wandering about the neighborhood in nightgown and fuzzy slippers confirm the allegation. If those sleep-enhancing drugs would enable me to dress in running shoes and flattering workout gear and exercise while I was unconscious, I'd request a prescription immediately.

Let's get back to 'bias'. Nobody's immune to it. Think you are? When was the last time you cheered for both teams when you were watching a sporting event? Never? Well then, you have home team bias. There's nothing wrong with certain biases. Love green but can't tolerate brown? Color bias is your friend. Enjoy coworkers but hate your boss? You guessed it, authority bias. Some biases are inane. Others are destructive and insulating. Fear and uncertainty cause bias. Don't understand something? Do you try to understand? If yes, then you can knock down the bias wall. Judge or condemn something out of hand? You're biased. Only listen to or associate with people who think like you? That's confirmation bias. No, not bias toward one of the Catholic sacraments that enlists you in a spiritual army. Think about it; chew on it or put it in your pipe and smoke it. I won't bore you with more details.

Amelia dear, why are you so obsessed with bias? The little voice, my subconscious, not my unconscious, is a slice of my inquiring mind. Think about it. I have three children; each unique. They're unconventional. That means they don't fit into those round holes on the pegboard of life. No hammer will ever pound their square, triangle or other non-circular shape into the hole of conformance.

Randy and his oldest sister are different from the conventional. I know they've opened themselves to being ridiculed, marginalized and discriminated against. But they've also opened themselves to the possibility off living authentically. Call me biased towards the unconventional and I'll tell you you're right, or left, or whatever direction works for you. I'm not partial to any direction but I don't support the wrong one.

Being authentic is not going along like life is one huge sleepwalk. I've heard a few people say they don't want to make waves. That's strange since waves start with a ripple or a butterfly flapping its wings. Sounds silly that a butterfly can cause a ripple in the ocean, right? Suppose you're the butterfly and making an impression on someone is the equivalent of flapping your wings. Even if you're unconscious, you make an impression. You can't avoid it. People will notice if you shut down. You may not hear it directly but you'll be the topic of conversation regardless.

"Hey, did you see Fred? The boss walked up one side of him and down the other. Fred's asleep at the switch. Do you think he likes being abused by his boss? Doesn't look like it matters."

Churning under the surface of Fred's sleepy disposition is the acid of frustration, making Fred wonder why he's there. Unconscious is like beauty; it's only skin deep. Fred's probably a disappointment to himself or someone important in his life. No, not his boss. If he was important to his boss, the ogre wouldn't treat him badly. Trying to beat production out of a person is about as useful as a raincoat in a shower.

Don't be unconscious. You'll miss so many challenging and wonderful things life can offer. Don't close your mind to learning experiences. What you refuse to learn today will be a missed opportunity to advance yourself professionally and personally. It's up to you.

Pass the Butter

Fans and Numbers

I'm not much for sports. I go along with my hubby, who enjoys watching grown men running around in pajamas chasing baseballs. He also likes watching grown men hit and chase each other around on large grass-equivalent surfaces or solid ice wearing things that make them look like aliens while old men in zebra stripes try to keep them in line.

You guessed it, I'm the occasional fan. Sometimes I'm a heater; when personal summers visit. Are you catching my drift about the word 'fan'? It's another example of the vagaries of the English language. A fan is a device with multiple blades that spins at varying speeds to move air. Do sports fans move air? They probably do it as a byproduct of consuming barley-based beverages, long tubes filled with meat-like substances and other solids and liquids that aid in the production of methane. I try not to be around when these fans start to move air!

I have nothing bad to say about sports fans. They pay, so adults can play kids games and make ungodly amounts of money. I don't own any paraphernalia with a logo. Ralph has Phillies, Eagles and Flyers gear. He wears it when the sports are in season. Because there is overlap between football and hockey, he wears football gear on weekends and hockey gear on weekdays.

I'm fascinated by the volume of people who profess loyalty to sports teams. I guess it has something to do with the need to belong. I belong to the human race but I don't wear any human race logo fashion. I know my loyalties. I'm loyal and cheer for my family. We don't have a family crest or anything that screams Ciracco. Even if a Ciracco logo existed, I'm not sure I'd wear it. Why do I care to tell people of my loyalty? More importantly, why would people care? *Oh look, there goes one of the Ciraccos. It must be cool to be one of them.*

There's another reason I don't advertise; I don't get paid. There's something backwards about the whole sports team advertisement. People pay good money to advertise teams that take that hard-earned money all the way to the bank. It's a big business. There is an important, self-preservation reason too. I've seen and heard of too many instances where people have been beaten for professing loyalty. Makes me wonder about people. *You like that team? That must mean you hate my team. You're the enemy. I'm gonna kick your ass.* Stupidity in action; makes me all warm and fuzzy all over.

Do what you will. Support whatever sports team turns you on. Be smart, don't wander into a crowd of opposing jerseys unless they're cows. Otherwise, you risk your life for what? It's not like the team's going to show up and defend you. That would be cool; but it would be tiring for the team members.

Fan gear is a huge draw. I think sales of team gear is more than a billion-dollar industry. Makes me wonder where all that money comes from. In Ralph's case, almost every article of clothing, from hat to jersey, shirt to gloves, were birthday or Christmas gift. I guess there's some benefit to having easy gifts. I've never been good at what to buy for the man who doesn't have everything.

Part of the fan gear phenomena is the obsession with being number one. How could every fan who buys a foam hand with pointer finger extended or license plate frame that states "#1 Fan" be number one? They all can do number 1, unless they have urinary tract problems, but it's not possible to have a bazillion number one fans. There isn't even a competition to determine who gets to sport that designation. That would be something. It might even rival the wing bowl.

Maybe the systems could change to consecutively number those items so we can keep track of the number of fans who desire to be counted. On second thought, those foam hands might become too large if they had to hold a seven-digit number. Probably not a good idea. I'd never wear anything that indicated ranking. I'd be afraid of a fight. I could imagine a rabid fan see my #1 designation and take offense and want to fight. Risking life and limb to be able to boast my biological capability is silly.

Since I brought it up, we've got to talk about that Philly tradition called the Wing Bowl. Sounds like a soup dish that holds chicken wings but it's not. It's an oddity that draws people to watch self-consumed people compete to eat the most chicken wings in the allotted time. No time to enjoy. Grab a wing, insert in mouth, bite down and strip the bone, chew quickly, swallow, repeat. Yep, no time to taste, enjoy or savor. You get to be champion wing eater if you make a bigger pig of yourself than the next person. The competition does have one thing going for it. The Wing Bowl isn't male dominated. There's a woman's division and a men's division. Everyone knows women are daintier than men and wouldn't ever dream of trying to best a man at eating. I can eat like the ship's going down but I could never best my husband.

Plus, there are scantily clad young women dancing about attracting the lust and desire of beer-greased libidos. They're called cheerleaders. They're leading cheers for the competitive eaters. I'll admit, cheering for someone to eat themselves into vomiting isn't enticing enough to get me to pay for the privilege. Ralph did invite me to join him and his buddies. Told me a few of the wives had agreed to go. I trusted him. I think the other women were there in surveillance mode.

Hubby went once. He said it bothered him to see all that food being consumed when he had to step over homeless people on the way to the stadium. Was it fear of avarice or embarrassment? I asked. He struggled for an answer. He'd probably go back if he wasn't feeling guilty about the homeless people. I know this because he mentioned the cheerleaders several times. I reminded him he had daughters who weren't far from their age. He didn't appreciate my insinuation. I wasn't worried about his reaction. He knew he was permitted his childish dalliances. All men look; wishing to touch. But they wouldn't know what to do with a woman twenty or more years their junior if she dropped naked into their lap.

Men have vivid imaginations; images of Tarzan and Jane. Loincloths and big muscles. Most men wouldn't qualify as Tarzan and few girls would fit Jane's profile. What would a young vixen want with a father figure? No, I'm not kidding. I've heard the stories of women chasing daddy figures. Could men not see the ulterior motive while brushing aside *their* ulterior motive? Some people are blind to the fact that sex doesn't equal love and lust does not equal undying devotion.

Woman: Like, Oh, my God, he's like so, like sexy. He's got this really, really, I mean like, superfast car. And, like all the other girls are, oh my God, actually so jealous! (Imagine long blond hair lifted by the air rushing over the open cabin of the six-figure convertible hurtling down a winding mountain road in the French Alps.)

Man: she's hot (imagines himself naked in Charles Atlas' body and woman swooning at the sight of him)

Pass the Butter

Identification by Political Affiliation

I heard an actor, in character, ask why people identify themselves by political party affiliation. The question started the wheels turning; the squealing and grinding told of rusty gears and infrequently used levers.

Is calling yourself Democrat, Republican, Independent a logical way of defining you? I didn't give it much thought until I heard the question. Made me wonder if I believed in and agreed with everything the political party nailed to their platform. Calling myself a political party member placed me in a box with a label to be filed with all the other identically labeled boxes. Think about it. If and when your political party does something that doesn't sit well with you, does your affiliation rub you wrong?

A political party is a strange phrase. Is politics a party and who's footing the bill? You wanna go to the political party? Bring your checkbook and your voter registration card. You can make a contribution (not tax deductible) to a party and you can vote to help determine which group gets to have the big blowout party.

Parties end. So how have these political parties hung around so long? Beats the stuffing out of me. And I've got considerable stuffing. More people keep showing up for the party. I think that leads to excess. Some people who attend the party stay too long. When it looks like your dentures are going to need another application of adhesion caulk, that should be the signal to say good night. The party boss seems to have too much power – kinda like the Cake Boss.

Now there's this relatively new thing called The Tea Party. Call me crazy, but didn't its namesake take place in a harbor in Massachusetts three centuries ago? Everything that old becomes new. I wish that was the case with my body. Maybe if we can get enough of the people attending the Tea Party onto that boat, we can cut the anchor loose and sail them away. That would end one of the parties. All we'd need to do is crash the others and get all the hungover party goers to agree to leave. You don't have to go home, but you can't stay here.

You haven't thought about it or don't care. I understand. There's nothing wrong with following; as long as what's ahead isn't a cliff or a brick wall. Party officials define the party; its rhetoric, beliefs and mission. I'm not a fan of allowing someone to decide for me. There's enough of that going on with politics and at work. I don't get consulted about every decision that impacts me. I understand. I don't have enough time to live the little slice of life I can manage. If I had to make every decision about every ingredient that went into the cake the politicians or the bosses were baking, I think I'd be nuttier than a jar of peanut butter.

Ralph and I have deep discussions sometimes. These topics inevitably come up. He's stoic.

"Are you happy with the change in the health insurance laws?" I asked.

"Do they impact us?" He always skipped to the end when he didn't think there was anything to gain.

"They might; if we didn't have insurance from our jobs."

"But we do have insurance from work."

"What about all the people who don't?"

"Does the new plan give them insurance?"

"Nothing *gives* them anything." This was where our conversations usually diverged.

"Amelia, if you could change the law how would you do it?" His logic put me on the spot. That usually spelled the end of discussions. I'd take the conversation in a different direction to not surrender.

"Do you consider yourself Democrat, Republican or Independent?"

"Yep."

"Yep, what?"

"Yep, I consider myself one of those."

"Which one?"

"Depends on the issue." I shot him a puzzled look.

"You're saying you don't identify with only one?"

"Why should I? There's no prize at the bottom of their Cracker Jack box. And, I get nothing for putting my political eggs in only one basket." He was reading my puzzled look.

"Isn't it easier to choose one?"

"And let politicians think I follow them blindly?" He had a solid point. "Are you loyal to one party regardless of their stance on the issues?"

"Nope. I have no reason to be tied to one party."

"So why are we discussing this?" Always the tough questions.

"Because I get frustrated when people talk about the sanctity of the two-party system."

"Sanctity is for the religious or the sanctimonious." I laughed, he was right. "I wouldn't get hung up on labels. We had this conversation when we talked about Suzanne and Randy." He was bringing the conversation around to smaller slices of life that we could influence.

"You're talking about change."

"That's right. Putting trust in the government to do the right thing only works when government takes its lead from the people. Government reacts and people who were waiting for the bandwagon jump on. Those people on the bandwagon who disagree, jump off. That's politics, sports, education, you name it." The man read people better than I did. He also dismissed things he couldn't influence.

"You think I put too much thought into things that I can't control."

"Don't you?" His eyebrows raised and his palms were upturned.

"Maybe." I wasn't going to concede yet.

"If you say so. But I'll always worry about Suzanne and Randy. Lisa's another story." I tried to sound convincing. He knew I was the queen of worry. He didn't want to be king over that kingdom.

Pass the Butter

Roxy Retires

Our dog gave us wonderful memories and unconditional love. It didn't matter our mood or disposition, our four-legged family member never held a grudge and rarely barked except to alert us to a visitor or to voice her enthusiasm. I waxed nostalgic. It beat waxing to remove body hair. Roxy died after fifteen years of loyal service. Sounds like she was one of the maids. I should have said fifteen years of love and affection. I wanted to think we returned that love and affection. Truthfully, we didn't. There were times when we were tired or sick; not to be confused with sick and tired.

Roxy had a safe place; her kennel. She liked to lay there surrounded by bars and in the company of a few tired but welcome toys and my weathered beach blanket that she loved. It took me a whole to realize her retreat was a signal to me to dial it back or get over myself. My temper never rose to anything beyond raising my voice. I don't think she appreciated loud noises. My shouting sent her scurrying to the kennel. Other loud noises like thunder sent her to the master bedroom where she took refuge under the bed.

She could predict bad weather because she'd find the bedroom before heavy rain. I'm not sure how she sensed it but she was more reliable than the weather person. Maybe they should have hired her. I giggled at the thought of her teaming with Punxsutawney Phil and predicting snow and rain. They would have made a cute and furry duo.

I told stories about how she would let us know when someone was at the front door. She also freaked out if we left her home. I couldn't fault her for having separation anxiety. I teared up more than once thinking about how she was taken from her mother and brothers when she was six weeks old. Ralph and I talked about reuniting the family but the boys had already been sold to other families and I wasn't interested in inviting strangers to our house for an event that may have meant nothing to any of the dogs.

The last three years of life slowed her down. She didn't run or chase as much. She lost the desire to herd and she spent more time on the sofa with Ralph or me. I think she knew what was coming and was giving us what was left for her to give. A few times my husband caught me hugging her and sobbing. He joined us in a group hug and tried to cheer me up. There wasn't anything he could say to make her end of life easier. I know he suffered through his dog's death when he was a teen. Maybe that made Roxy's farewell tour easier on him. Fortunately she didn't suffer; according to the vet. I'm not sure how he knew unless he was related to the pet whisperer.

When it was her time to go, we made her as comfortable as we knew how. Death was a state of being we wanted to be without. We dreaded the thought of taking her to the vet to put her down. I didn't want to be the one to make the call. Ralph was ambivalent; he didn't want her to suffer just so we could feel better about not making the call. Fortunately for us she died in her sleep. Ralph found her lying peacefully in the kennel. When he told me I broke down and cried. There was no consoling me. She was one of the kids and a wonderful addition to the family. I had flashbacks to the days before she arrived. I had been tough about bringing another living thing into our crazy house. In typical Amelia style, I beat myself up for harboring those thoughts fifteen years ago. I told you Sicilians have long memories.

Pass the Butter

"What do we tell people when they ask where she is?"

"Tell them she died," Ralph said.

"Shouldn't we be softer? Shouldn't we say she passed away?" Soft wasn't an adjective anyone who knew me would mistakenly use to describe me.

After my husband wiped the sarcasm from his face he replied, "Passing away is something a quarterback without a running game does."

"Huh?" He threw me when he used sports analogies.

"Just say she died peacefully." I nodded to accept his compromise.

Roxy wasn't out and about much the last few months of life. One of the neighbors asked about Euthanasia. "Are you going to have her euthanized?"

"What?"

"Euthanized. Are you going to euthanize her?" Harry was a strange duck, literally, He looked like Daffy Duck with a long nose emulating a duck's bill, short forehead and thinning hair he colored jet black and slicked back.

"We'll probably have it done after we Simonize her. Then afterwards, we'll memorize then eulogize, we'll hypothesize and memorialize. But we would never minimize." I stopped to give Harry a chance to process. "Really Harry, Euthanasia? Sounds like young people in China or Indonesia." He looked at me like I was speaking a foreign language. I knew I confused him; he didn't get the play on words.

"That's what they call it," he replied defensively.

"And just who are they?"

"You know." He tried to sound convincing.

"If I knew, do you think I'd ask?"

"I don't know."

"Exactly." I left him to untangle the word knots I had tied. When I walked through the front door I almost doubled over laughing at my foolishness. I don't think Harry appreciated me but I appreciated him for lifting the dark cloud, if only for a moment.

"What are you laughing about?" Ralph walked in from the garage.

"Something really silly."

"You don't say." His eyes narrowed as he dug into the fridge for a beer."

"You gonna drink alone?" That question caused him to do a double take.

"You want one of these?" He held up a long neck.

"No, I was inquiring so I could record your response in my research database." His shoulders dropped. I think he wished he had stayed in the garage. He handed me one of the bottles and stared at me for a couple of beats. He was about to take a pull.

"Wait, we need to toast." That brought skepticism to his face in technicolor.

"What are we celebrating," he asked; trying to sound sincere.

"Roxy of course." At the sound of her name she raised her head and appeared to smile before returning her head to her favorite red pillow on the sofa. I thought I detected a tear in the corner of Ralph's eye. Maybe it was the tears blurring my vision.

Pass the Butter

All in All and Other Musings

Is 'all' in 'all'? Of course, it is. 'All' is in all. It's a simple three-letter word that only has the capacity to house a few words, such as: all, a, al, and la. So if 'all' is in 'all', what's the benefit of acknowledging? Maybe it begs the question if 'all' is in 'all', is it also in other words? Let's investigate. "All" is in: stall, fall, ball, mall, shall, wall, call, gall, pall, tall, and a few other words. I'm sure you'll think of several others to add to the list.

What does the phrase 'all in all' mean? According to Miriam Webster, it means "Considering Everything". I'm not sure we could live long enough to consider *everything*. I've heard the phrase used in a song, something about feeling ten feet tall and someone so bright they were named Sunny.

Ralph and I were walking. I used to call it 'taking a walk', until I asked Ralph, "You wanna take a walk?"

"Where are we taking it?"

"Outside."

"I know that. Are we taking it somewhere?"

"Huh?" He had a way of confusing the simplest things.

"We're taking a walk around the neighborhood."

"Is that where the walk wants to go?"

"Ugh! You're impossible."

"It's possible, but I'm not sure the walk is interested in going around the neighborhood."

"Okay Webster, how would you ask the question?"

"How about 'up for a walk'.

"Great. But suppose I'm down. Either on the floor or on the sofa or on my luck?"

"That's good Meel. These conversations are so enlightening."

I thought I'd try another approach since runway 9 Left was closed. "So are you interested in walking?"

"Yes, let's."

"You mean let's walk?" He left me no choice but to be a needle. Without responding verbally, he sat on the sofa after grabbing his walking shoes and slipped them on.

After standing, her replied, "I'm up for a walk." I passed up the opportunity to continue the sparkling repartee. Moments later we were out the door. It felt weird walking without Roxy in tow. She would have been walking dutifully beside Ralph. We had scrapped the leash long ago. Roxy usually did her business in the back yard and wasn't a threat to run off.

The evening air was fresh after a drenching rain. I wishing I had worn my blue rain shoes. Ralph's soiled walking shoes were a pair of beat up sneakers that had been white originally. Now they were a dingy gray with scuff marks and paint drippings. I tried to encourage him to invest in a new pair. He showed me the bottoms and proclaimed there was plenty of tread left.

"This is romantic," I said, pulling tightly to his arm before releasing. I looked at him for a reply. He appeared lost in thought. "Nickel for your thoughts." I stopped saying 'penny for your thoughts' after Ralph told me I needed to consider inflation.

"This is good. I forgot how peaceful the neighborhood is after a storm." I was expecting more enthusiasm. I should have known better. Ralph could have been crowned Count Understatement. I admired the extensive landscaping bordering some of the homes. A few people had decided to remodel their homes rather than move; adding large additions that made the building appear estate-like. I understood. The neighborhood was established and property values were solid. I felt a twinge of regret that I hadn't invested time in our sparse planting beds. After a moment the regret passed.

"Why do you think they call it standing water?" I had been examining a few puddles that formed in depressions in the sidewalk.

"Because it's not running." My answer man had a comeback for everything.

"How can you tell it's standing and not leaning or sitting or lying down?"

"Yeah."

"So why isn't it called 'sitting water'?"

"I don't know. When we get home you can research it." He knew my desire to surf the internet was about as great as my desire for gardening.

"I'm going to call it 'sitting water' because it's just sitting there.

"You go right ahead." He took my hand and held it firmly. It was his way of showing he loved me no matter how silly I got.

We walked for about thirty minutes before we flopped on the sofa in the Family Room. When Roxy was still with us, she would have taken up her spot on the second sofa to our left. I tried wash the memory away to keep from experiencing Armageddon. Ralph woke the television; I think he sensed my emotional trough.

"Wanna watch something stupid?"

"You mean something with potty humor?" He rolled his eyes. "Sure, why not. I could use a good or bad laugh." He wrapped an arm around my shoulder and handed me the remote.

"You drive." I leaned back and looked at him out of the corner of my eye.

"You feeling okay?"

"Why?"

"You never surrender the remote."

"Never say never." Using absolutes was another thing he like to debunk. I called up the on-screen guide and scrolled through the channels. After several minutes of fruitless searching I handed the remote back to my husband.

"Find something on one of the movie services. And remind me to cancel the cable subscription. Eighty bucks a month and there's nothing on." I pushed myself off the sofa. "I'm going to make popcorn. You want anything?"

"I'll share the popcorn. How about a couple of beers?"

"You do the beer and I'll do the popcorn." I had invested in a glass popcorn popper that worked in the microwave. I bought on line. It was made by Corning and worked really well. There weren't many unpopped kernels and I didn't have to add oil to the unpopped kernels. I didn't want to be too healthy so I drenched the popped corn with melted salted butter. What's popcorn without butter and salt? Healthy!

Pass the Butter

Hugged and Loved

We hugged our kids; even when they were teens. When they were toddlers, they loved to snuggle; teens not so much. Hugging is a way many nationalities express feelings. Italians enjoy hugging and kissing. Not in the way you're thinking. Even the men embraced. Italian males didn't call if hugging. That was for the women.

Hugging is underrated. The 'man up' generation hides behind machismo. What are they hiding? I'm glad you asked. They're hiding their softer side. Some guys can't deal with being soft. They insist it's weakness to show emotions. Oh, it's okay to show anger. What? Anger's not an emotion? Now I know you're hallucinating. Ralph has a few male friends who subscribe to the theory that men must always be strong. Let the women be weak. I've recommended they cancel their subscription to macho man weekly.

Women are weak. How else would you explain enduring child birth, multiple times! We'll also touch on diaper changing, removing vomit and other bodily fluids after an unscheduled evacuation. Those are definitely acts of the faint of heart, right?

I struggle trying to understand. I know, I'm wasting precious time and burning my dwindling supply of neurons trying to solve something even Sherlock Holmes wouldn't attempt. If more people expressed genuine G-rated affection, the world would be a better place. An actor once said, "More people should give from the heart." I don't think h meant blood;

although some people try to draw blood and they're not medical professionals.

My husband experienced a few of those macho men at the office. They had something to prove to themselves. Ralph didn't seem to care and that probably rubbed them the wrong way. People like that can't be rubbed the right way even if they came with a map and instructions. H rarely revealed those wonderfully educational encounters. He wasn't much for discussing things he couldn't control. When he walked away, guys gave up on him figuring him for a lesser man because he didn't agree with them. On the few occasions when a guy would get in his face, Ralph would take a step back and calmly say, "You probably weren't hugged enough when you were a child. But there's still time." Based on the reaction he got, hubby didn't think the recipient understood the nuanced implication. He had a way with understatement.

Ralph and his brother embrace when they greet each other. I saw him do the same with a couple of motorcycle buddies. The non-embracers seemed to stiffen when they saw their friends close. I wonder if they thought maybe the men were doing this because they were attracted to each other. If they were thinking that; I wouldn't want to be around them. Guilty by innuendo or prejudice didn't float my boat.

"Why do Mike and Ernie seem to back away when you and George hug?"

"You mean embrace?"

"I mean hug. Stop trying to manify your actions."

"Manify. Did you can 'manify'?"

"Yep." My course in urbanization was working.

"Never heard that term. Does it mean what I think it means?"

"What do you think it means?" I was beginning to sound like a game show hostess or a psychologist.

"That I try to put a manly spin on things."

"You're pretty smart for a guy."

"I married you, didn't I?"

"I think your mother thought you lost a few marbles in college."

"I never played marbles." I could see this was headed towards a brick wall at lightning speed.

"Even so, I still think you're smart." He kissed me playfully before settling back into the sofa.

"Mike and Ernie had a few bad experiences." I wasn't sure where this was going or how we got here. "They have emotional baggage."

"Did they leave it on the plane?" He smirked.

"I'm serious. Those guys have been in therapy."

"And they're on two wheels terrorizing quiet neighborhoods."

"I think you need to cut them a break."

"It's that serious?" I wasn't trying to be evil. The caustic remarks seemed to be on autopilot.

"I wouldn't talk about it if it wasn't."

"What exactly happened?" He paused and studied the palms of his hands.

"I shouldn't share their secret." I wasn't going to encourage him. If he was going to share, it was going to be all his doing. "If I tell you anything about them, you've got to swear to secrecy." I caught his stare; it was heavy and hard.

"Does that include posting it on Facebook?" He stood abruptly and thrust his hands hard into his pockets and began to pace.

"Damn it Amelia, why must you make light of every situation?" I was torn between contrition and laughing uncontrollably. I think I might have taken too many happy pills. After swallowing what was left of attitude I conjured up a sober expression.

"I promise not to say anything to anybody." He was swearing me to total secrecy. Maybe it had something to do with my keeping secrets, about the kids, from him. Maybe he really trusted me with a secret. Maybe I was going to be nominated for sainthood.

"Want a beer?" That was his way of getting a short recess from the proceedings.

"No, I'll pass." I wasn't a big beer drinker. I wasn't even a little beer drinker. It didn't matter the size of the beer; I wasn't a regular drinker. He returned to the Family Room with a long neck, looking pale. I think he might have gone too far offering to disclose something that was apparently off limits to the world. I was curious to at least know why they trusted him enough to share with my husband.

"You don't have to tell me anything. This isn't something that's important to our relationship." He seemed unsettled; like this secret somehow had attached itself to him like a parasite. The beer bottle was empty after the second pull. His actions screamed nervousness. My thoughts shifted to needing to know. This could and apparently would come between us. He paced like an expectant father uncertain of the success of the birthing process.

He stopped, turned and stared down at me. I blinked twice and caught myself holding my breath. "Okay, here goes." He paused. "Promise you'll let me finish before you say anything."

"I promise." This was going to be hard. He hesitated. I think he wanted another drink to steady himself.

"You know I went to an all-boys high school." I nodded. I had gone to an all-girls high school. That's where it started and probably how it started."

"When, what?" His stare told me to be quiet.

"I was a sophomore, so were you." Was it something between us, something I did? "Most of the teachers were priests; only a few lay teachers."

"Same in my school, more nuns than lay." This time he didn't try to stop my response.

"I lost a lot of friends that year." The worry machine was shifting into second gear. "Billy, Larry, Alex, Joe and Ernie all walked away from me." His shoulders slumped as he talked. I tried to remember those days but memory was foggy; almost like those days were erased from my memory.

"Sophomore year was a tough one for both of us." There was no acknowledgement in his expression.

"I told this to those guys and they almost laughed me out of existence." Emotional pain radiated from him.

"But you didn't lose all your friends."

"I didn't. But losing one was bad. Losing those guys was really bad. I thought we were tight. I guess I was wrong." Fragments of memory began to filter back.

"I remember we weren't so close for a few months."

"I almost walked away from you." The conversation just crossed the threshold from threatening to ominous.

"I'd glad you didn't." I started to rise. I wanted to hug him. He stopped me with the wave of a hand. Dropping back into the sofa I was feeling alone.

"I trusted those guys. They always told me they had my back. I was an idiot; thinking they meant what they said."

"They were shallow. You didn't deserve that."

"Well, I got it and it made me want to dry up and blow away." Holy shit, he pulled vulnerability out of the closet and was running it up the emotional flagpole.

"I've never seen you like this."

"I never thought it would surface. I tried to bury it and I thought I did. But it's back and I have to tell you."

"Tell me what?" I rose from the sofa again. This time I ignored his stop sign. At first. he resisted my hug. Then he pulled me into him so tightly I thought I might come out the other side.

"The priests… One priest… Was preying on some of us." My mind went blank before it erupted with angry fireworks.

"What?" I screamed loud enough to chatter crystal. He turned away, ashamed.

"I feel like I betrayed you and myself."

"Wait. Priests were using you?"

"And some of the other guys."

"What did you do? Who did you tell?" He glared at me; the hard stare back.

"Who was I gonna tell? My mother was in love with the church. She thought the priests walked on water."

"Those were shallow puddles." I wanted to choke somebody and I had an idea where to start.

"I didn't think anyone would believe me."

"What about the others?"

"They were just as scared as me. Besides, I didn't know there were others until senior week."

"Why was senior week so special?"

"We got drunk and the secret just came out." He sounded ashamed as he turned away.

"Oh Ralph, I'm so sorry." I tried to hug him but he shrugged me off. I don't harbor ill feelings much but I began to hate the priests at his high school. They knew nobody would rat them out. Back then, you disrespected a teacher or, God forbid, a priest or a nun and our parents would give us what for. Besides, the priest would deny and their parents might think them liars or worse. I don't know how he hid the thing for so long.

"How did you hide it for so long? I had no idea." He shrugged and sat down hard in his easy chair.

"Do you love me less?"

"Less than what?"

"You know."

"No, I don't."

"Maybe I should have fought back. Maybe I should have said something."

"Like at that age you didn't care what people thought or the damage you'd do to your reputation."

He paused to gather himself. "I'm so sorry I didn't tell you before I asked you to marry me."

"Do you honestly think that would have made any difference?"

"I don't know." He spoke to the television.

"Randolph William Ciracco. How dare you think I would have run away from you if you told me." A sardonic smile formed on his lips. "I don't think we need to talk about this any longer. I don't want this to cloud our marriage." I walked around the coffee table and stood in front of my husband. "Son of a bitch pedophile. If I could get my hands on the bastard I'd make him regret all the shit he pulled on you and your friends." My temper was spiking; my face red. Ralph looked up at me.

"You're gonna have a heart attack or bust a blood vessel."

"Let me say what I need to say to get it out of my system."

"Go ahead, you're gonna say it anyway." My eyes burned with rage. I wanted to kill somebody. Here I was worried about the kids and all the while my husband was scarred by people we were supposed to trust. The whole thing made me sick. I had to do something to distract myself so I moved to the kitchen and began taking the dishes out of the dishwasher and washing them. Don't ask me why.

Ralph wandered in. I guess it was all the clanging of glasses and crashing of dishes.

"Dishwasher broken?"

"Not like I'd like to break somebody and feed his sorry ass to the piranhas."

"We don't have piranhas. We don't even have a fish tank."

"It was a figure of speech."

"I figured as much." The more he worked to lighten my mood, the more difficult it was for me to carry the grudge. He hugged me and I kissed him with the passion of youth. After a few minutes of tongue wrestling I stepped back.

"I guess you don't want me to kill anybody. I could you know. I have a few friends."

"Oh yeah? Do I know any of these killer friends?"

"Maybe." Those were the last words spoken before we melted into each other and enjoyed slow and satisfying sex.

Pass the Butter

For Free

YOU'VE HEARD THOSE WORDS. "Get it for free." 'For free' has a verbose ring to it. 'For free' really means 'for the benefit of free'. Isn't it really for the recipient's benefit? If it's for the benefit of 'free', then I think free needs to get it for themselves. Who is this 'free' person anyway? Are they helpless? Do they have this massive following that everyone wants to get something for them? Are they the pied piper of free? Get information 'for free'. Get this tote bag 'for free'. Maybe people feel sorry for free. I've been thinking about whether I knew anybody named 'free'. I even asked my husband.

"I knew of a basketball player named 'Free'. He changed his first name to 'World Be'." Maybe people felt sorry for him and wanted him to have legions of pens and tote bags and other things he may not have been capable of obtaining. If everyone got one of the 'for free' items for World Be, where would he put them? He'd need a warehouse to store them. Suppose he ran out of room and things kept showing up? Would he have to throw them away? If that was the case, sending all those things to 'Free' would end up costing him time and money to collect, store or throw them away. So much trash would come from a good deed that I'm not sure it would be worth it.

All joking aside, we have this need to add words when they do nothing to improve the message. Maybe if we had a preposition moratorium, we might be better positioned to communicate the message.

I also love the statement 'free gift'. Aren't gifts free? Wouldn't it be a knee slapper at a birthday party or Christmas (there's that politically incorrect word again) to give a gift and ask for something in return? I'm not talking about a thank you or a smile or a kiss. They're chump change. I'm talking something more substantial; like a client reference or a promise to be named in a will. I might go as far as asking for a loan. Gifts cost money and there's never enough to go around.

Then there's the 'free, no obligation' offers. If there was an obligation, the thing wouldn't be free. In Amelia's English, free means no strings or obligations attached. Attach a string or an obligation and 'free' goes out the window with the bath water.

The sales pitch that includes: buy one and get this tote bag free. Wait, buy something and get something free? I was tempted to call for the free gift even if I didn't buy the overpriced offering.

"Hi, I saw your ad on television."

"Which one?"

"The one that just ran on channel 378 on my cable network."

"Ma'am, we run lots of commercials on lots of cable channels."

"So you're not the company?"

"No ma'am, we're the company that takes the orders."

"Oh, I see." I'm sure the agent was happy to her about my vision acuity. I proceeded to describe the product. She was able to find it in her computer system.

"I'd like the free tote."

"Sure, all I need to do is get your payment information, including your address."

"Payment information, isn't the tote bag free?"

"You have to buy the product to get the tote bag."

"So the tote bag isn't free?"

"It's free if you buy the product."

"Wait. I buy something to get something free."

Pass the Butter

"That's correct." She was starting to sound annoyed.

"Then the cost of the tote bag is included in the cost of the item."

"Ma'am, are you interested in buying the toaster oven?"

"I already have a toaster oven. In fact, I have two of them. "One belongs in the trash but my husband insists on trying to fix it. But he won't listen and I'm tired of trying to tell him." I was getting the feeling the operator was getting tired of me. "I'm interested in the free tote bag."

"I'm sorry you don't need the toaster oven. Is there anything I can help you with?" I think she needed a hearing aid.

"Not if I can't get the free tote bag."

"You can't without buying the toaster oven." Her speech was clipped and harsh.

"Are we on a recorded line? Hello?" I think she hung up. I could have really used that tote bag.

They were selling one of those gadgets to make housework simpler. I watched the infomercial and thought this would be something I'd buy even if there wasn't a free tote bag. The advertisement got better when they offered to double the deal if I paid separate shipping and handling. I got the shipping part. But I was going to be doing the handling when I received it so why would I want to pay someone else to handle it unless they were going to handle it around my house and save me the effort. I thought so much of the product that I called the number on the screen. The guy doing the sales pitch made it clear I had to call within ten minutes to get the double order. I'm not sure if he really had a stop watch on the call time but I was able to get through before the timer on the television get to seven minutes.

"Hello, I'm calling about that flexible duster thing."

"Yes, the miracle duster."

"Is it really only $9.95?"

"That's right."

"And I get a second one free?"

"Yes, just pay separate shipping and handling."

"Can I just pay the shipping? I'll be handling them when they get here."

"No ma'am. The handling is the cost to get it from the warehouse and prepare it for shipping."

"Oh, I didn't know."

"No problem. Can I get your information?"

"How much is shipping and handling?"

"For the first item it's $7.95."

"And the second item?"

"$7.95."

"Are they coming from the same warehouse?"

"I don't know. I don't work at the warehouse."

"Do you think they would?"

"I really don't know." I think she *did* know and wasn't sharing.

"Is the stock person going to get my orders at the same time?"

"Ma'am, I don't know." I think she was about to say "I don't care", but she caught herself.

"It's important that I know. This way if they grab two of the dusters at the same time and put them in the same box, I could save the second shipping and handling charge."

"Ma'am, do you want to order the items?"

"Are we on a recorded line?" The phone went dead again. I wonder if it was the same call center? I thought about calling and telling them about the phone problems but they probably had too much work to do already.

I read a sign that said "No Smoking is permitted within this building." Taking it literally – I'm not sure how else to take something – the sign says that it's okay that you don't smoke in the building. I know that's not the message the sign was designed to convey. Unfortunately, spelling and grammar checking isn't ubiquitous. Makes me wonder who thought *that* construct was the best way to state the intent of a non-smoking building. There's another phrase I find amusing: A non-smoking building. The only ways the building could smoke if it was on fire, or it was a smoking hot building! I said it before but it's worth repeating. The English language and the construction of phrases, sentences and thoughts is confusing. Worse, I don't think people read what they write.

I love the latest phrase 'in all actuality'. That puzzled me for a few minutes. I burned precious brain cells trying to determine the levels of actuality. There's 'no actuality', that's either conjecture, fantasy or fiction. Is there "partial actuality'? Is that like being half right or half-baked? And isn't half right or half-baked really half wrong or undercooked? I couldn't figure why 'all actuality' was any different from plain old 'actuality'. Maybe it had something to do with 'plain old'. I guess change is good; especially when it's exact change or the correct amount of change.

Speaking of change, I know, I'm jumping around. It's my version of exercise! Ever buy something that costs $5.07 and give the cashier a ten-dollar bill? While the cashier is making change you dig seven cents or a dime out of your purse? How many times does that action cause the cashier to tense and appear confused? Mathematics without the aid of a calculator or cash register has become a relic of past generations.

Remember the days of the raised keys and the manual input of prices for purchases? In some establishments the numbers have been replaced by pictures of menu items. There's an elegance to having the multiple digit cost of an item entered with the push of one button. But it wasn't elegance that spurred the change. It was the findings of a consulting firm that the retailer was losing money because employees were charging the wrong price for menu items. The slippery slope to counting on fingers and toes was nurtured on the way to adulthood.

Pass the Butter

You Don't Say

    I speak my mind. You find that shocking? My friends laugh when I say what's on my mind. Some say I don't have a filter. I think filters are important, just not for people. Filters are for cigarettes and clothes dryers. I'm not advocating for being crass or rude. People should communicate respectfully; which doesn't mean holding back the truth.
    "But you'll hurt that person's feelings." One of my friends responded to my refusal to be al gooey and dripping sweet.
    "So I should lie to make them feel good?"
    "I'm not saying that?"
    "Then what are you saying?" I was getting exasperated.
    "You can be a little softer in your approach."
    "If I was any softer I'd be floating."
    She exhibited a wry smile. I knew I was about as soft as cured concrete but I did have my moments. I didn't drop buildings on people; only near them. The point is understanding what someone means. Vying for the master or mistress of understatement isn't attractive. Why? So glad you asked. If I have to spend time deciphering your message, I may as well apply to the NSA or other spy agency. I'm not a cryptographer. I'm not even a photographer.
    Say what you mean and hope people are paying attention and not fiddling with their electronic distraction devices. I think I just invented a new acronym: EDD. It's close to ADD for attention deficit disorder. EDDs contribute to or perpetuate

ADD. So if you have ADD, don't add an EDD to your already distracted state.

"Eli, why don't you think I have couth?"

"You're in your face."

"Well it's better than being in your wallet, like some of the smooth talkers. You know the ones that have slippery palms and suction cups on the tips of their fingers."

"Uh huh. You don't say. But don't you think that's a bit harsh?"

"It may be, but it's true."

"Uh, huh. You don't say. But again, you don't have to use the truth as a weapon."

Truth is a weapon to fight lies." I was trying to have a conversation with one of my older male colleagues. Every time I took a breath or paused, he'd say, "You don't say". And I would counter with a direct response. Then he would say, "Uh huh" in a tone that was part questioning and part deep analysis.

After the third 'don't say volley, I had to ask, "Why do you insist on saying that line?"

"What line?" I tried to read his expression to see if he was kidding.

"You don't say."

"What?"

"You say, you don't say, every time I say something."

"Do I?"

He looked skeptically at me. "You really don't know you're saying it?"

"I don't!" He sounded and acted astonished.

"Sounds like it bothers you."

"No more than running a cheese grater over my cheek." He looked puzzled.

"A cheese grater, huh? You don't say."

"Well, maybe one of those zesters." I tried to lighten the mood but I had already tossed the conversational grenade.

Pass the Butter

"Now that you mention it, maybe I don't realize I'm saying it." There's another one of those 'nails on the chalk board' moments. *Now that you mention it, you don't say.* I wasn't sure I could continue the conversation. If he lobbed another one of those pithy phrases I might scream.

"Oh, look at the time. Gotta go. So good talking to you Eli." He stood befuddled as I scurried away feeling less claustrophobic the further I got from him.

Ever give someone a piece of your mind? That's another gem of a phrase. Is that like a piece of cake? I don't understand the concept of giving someone a piece of your mind. What would the recipient do with it? If enough people gave someone a piece of their mind, would the person, fortunate enough to receive those pieces, would they be able to put them all together to make a whole mind? I guess that begs the question, how many pieces does it take to make a whole mind. Would you need to borrow the Vulcan powers of mind meld to get the pieces to stick? What if all those pieces were like pieces of a puzzle with different innies and outies? Would you toss pieces that didn't fit? What if those pieces held valuable insights into people, places or things?

Could you use pieces from the minds of others to replace the pieces you gave away? What about all those people who've given away pieces, are they now less mindful? Are those the people who can only 'give half a mind'? Maybe that's why some people do mindless things. They've given away all of their mind. A politician once said, "It's a terrible thing to lose one's mind." I agree, if you don't find it after you lose it. Is it equally as terrible to give it away? And will you get it back if you give it away?

Nikki DiCaro

Are there warning bells or sirens when you're about to give away too much mind? *Warning, warning, giving away another piece of your mind will bring your mind capacity below acceptable levels.* Can you retrieve pieces you gave away, kinda like replenishing your depleted mind? Can you visit the mind shelter to acquire mind segments? Can you select parts that will strengthen your mind? Or are you buying without knowing? Scares me to think people are wandering around with a partially empty mind cavity. If it's really a cavity, do you go to the mind doctor to fill it?

Are psychologists 'mind doctors'? Is that why they're called shrinks? Do they shrink your mind cavity so when you give away a piece of your mind, there isn't a yawning hole or gap in your mind? I worry about how this whole 'giving pieces of your mind' could impact the aging process. Do we become forgetful? Could this be a cause of mental disease or memory loss? Wow, I think I might have stumbled upon something. Am I stumbling because some of my mind is gone?

Pass the Butter

Property of ...

The other day I saw a woman on the train wearing a cute pink ball cap. I thought it was cute until I read the words on the marquee, "Property of" some strip club. Wait, I think they're called Gentlemen's club. I'll have a few things to say about that in a minute.

Why would anyone wear anything that shouted servitude? Being the property of another was supposed to have ended in 1865. Remember the end of slavery? Yet people proudly wear shirts, hats and other shameless advertisements that announce their being owned by a faceless organization. I don't think people consider what they wear. I get the message. It's one of belonging. Being owned by a professional team or a popular club screams inclusion and acceptance. Funny how the concept of freedom has devolved into the urgent need to belong at all costs.

I almost wanted to ask the woman what motivated her to tell people she was the property of another. She didn't look happy. My question might have tipped her further towards despair. If she felt the incredible need to be associated with another organization at any cost, who was I to convince her otherwise?

Thinking out loud, my appliances *are* my property. I wonder if they're happy being owned. If machines could rise up and rebel, would my appliances join the rebellion or announce their contentment with the living conditions? Given the age of some of the gadgets, they'd probably stay put because they weren't in any condition to endure the rough road to independence. There wouldn't be a big demand for their services if they were forced to make a go of it in the open market.

My appliances have it good. We're loyal and usually keep them until they die. We don't euthanize them or cast them aside. It's my husband more than me who has the loyal streak. I was in the market for newer models but he wouldn't hear of it. I think he had strong feelings of attachment. Come to think of it, attachment to money was probably the driving factor although looking in the garage, he did have a few relics from a couple of times when I was able to convince him to upgrade. Those appliances needed to be retired. I don't think they would have spoken ill of us if they could speak. Any appliance that had provided loyal service for twenty years would have been grateful to their owner.

I want my appliances to feel loved. This way they will happily perform their duties and we won't have to entertain replacing them.

***

Gentlemen's clubs are fascinating places. I thought they would be places to find gentlemen; a place where gentle women go to meet the perfect gentleman. It would be a safe place where conversation was respectful. Women would be demure and men would be chivalrous. Hints of alcohol and light fare would help ease any trepidation these single men and women would feel embarking upon the phenomenon of dating.

I couldn't be further away from the truth than if I was searching for the ocean in Oklahoma. Well Dorothy, you're not in Kansas anymore. Labeling these establishments as Gentlemen's clubs is like calling premeditated murder another form of love. I love you so much I need to have your life.

Pass the Butter

Please where men go to watch women do things for money; how innovative! These places, with names like Secrets, Risqué, Raw, Bare, etc. make a farce out of the term 'gentle". Naming a place with this clientele 'Secret' is probably not correct unless all the patrons wear masks or are sworn to secrecy under pain of death or something equally unsavory. If you have secrets before entering 'Secrets', I'm sure you won't have the same number of secrets when you leave.

Hey Charlie, how's it hanging?

Seriously Fred, if it's hanging now, I'm gonna need more than a lap dance to cure my man problem.

The 'man' thing I get. Boys will be boys and men will be children. This is where men, and some women, go to watch almost naked women dance around and collect dollars, propositions and thoughtfully colorful metaphors. Young females contort their bodies around poles and across lighted dance floors, doing things that separate patrons from their money. These dancers have bodies to die for. And if the men ever got their wish with these girls they'd probably keel over! The girls give lap dances while the men fantasize about doing things to women that their bodies probably couldn't deliver on a good day. Are men who go to clubs, married, single or betrothed, really gentlemen? I don't get the concept. I guess it's about justification. It may also be a way for married women, girlfriends and fiancés to justify letting their men go to fantasize.

I asked around at work. Some of the women thought it was harmless to let their husbands off the leash, as they put it. That's another conversation all together! Some women say their sexual experience with the husband is heightened after the gentleman has attended one of these shows. I wonder if he's thinking about his wife when they're intimate. Or, is he thinking about one or more of the women who danced on his lap and made parts of his body respond in ways that may have been absent in the bedroom?

Nikki DiCaro

Then there are, or were, the Chippendales. When I first heard of them I wondered why young women would pay to see old world furniture. Then I learned men with physiques too good to be real, performed for women who would swoon over them. Panties and bras would become sensual projectiles. I couldn't see throwing a perfectly good bra at people who wouldn't have man boobs to use them. The panties thing seemed so unsanitary. When I threw my panties in the laundry basket, sometimes I thought the basket wanted to throw them back.

I wasn't much for going without undergarments. Somebody called it 'going commando'. Unless combat uniforms for women were lined with premium cotton or silk, I didn't think female soldiers would risk irritation by going without panties. I thought about writing to the Pentagon to ask for clarification as to whether going commando was gender neutral. They were so busy down there dealing with trying to keep different parts of the world from erupting into civil war, that I decided against it.

I do remember a singer who had the same effect on women when he performed. Since he's aged, I wonder whether large, reinforced underwire bras and matron panties would still encourage him to perform.

The whole 'property of' thing will not be resolved to my satisfaction so I think I'll move to another burning topic.

Pass the Butter

Civil War?

War is a small word with many implications. *We're going to war, gentlemen.* I wonder if he was addressing the guys in the clubs. *This means war!* And here I thought 'this' meant 'this'. If 'this' means war, why would you need the word 'war'? I hope I'm not confusing you because I usually confuse myself. If you're up for a little word substitution, let's try it. Substitute 'this' with 'war'.

I'm so tired of this, becomes *I'm so tired of war*.

This makes me want to cry, becomes *War makes me want to cry*.

It works; you try it.

The words 'civil' and 'war' don't seem to go together. Can there be a civil war? Being civil means acting civilized. Does being civilized mean acting in a hostile manner? Looking around the world today, that might explain all the hostility, selfishness and bias. If you believe civil means acting civilized, then how do you run a war when you're trying to be civil?

"Charge that hill men, and kill everything in your path!"

"Excuse me captain, but is that the civilized thing to do? This is supposed to be a civil war."

"What are you flapping about, soldier?"

"I'm trying to understand."

"It's not your job to understand. Your job is to follow orders; my orders."

"But aren't we fighting a civil war?"

"We're fighting a war and you can't be civil in a war! Now charge that hill!"

"What did it do?"

"What are you babbling about now soldier?"

"Well captain, I'm a lawyer and before I can charge the hill with something, I need to know what the hill is being accused of."

"It's being accused of harboring the enemy, the uncivilized enemy!"

"Oh, now I understand. We're not fighting a civil war, we're fighting a war to restore civility."

The Civil War, also called the War Between the North and the South, probably began as a civil contest between family members, friends and relatives. But it soon escalated beyond the boundaries of civility. I think I'm beginning to understand.

I kinda get why wars need names. There have been so many, that without catchy names, we might forget all the energy that went into planning and executing attacks, counterattacks and all the other types of attacks. How would we distinguish between one war and another if there was nothing making them special?

Wars are really a shame. So many people dying, homes destroyed, way of life ruined, lives changed forever. I don't understand why men fight. I don't get why they have to fight in the first place. Of for that matter, the second or third places. Boys are taught to b rough and tough. We buy them soldiers and toy guns. We introduce them to competitive sports where winning is everything and losers have to endure shame. Angry, competitive boys turn to driven and conquering men. Not all competitive boys become warriors. Just like all petty thieves don't become bank robbers.

We never gave Randy those stereotypical boy toys and he never asked for them. At first, I was surprised his father didn't try to build a little man. I think he understood our children were unique and would form their lives through self-made experiences. Maybe that's why Randy enjoyed playing with girls more than boys. Girls were collaborative and not always competitive. Sure, girls could be caddy and moody. Boys could be argumentative and combative. Some people think if we had given Randy soldiers and guns and shamed him into football and baseball he might not be gay.

News flash people, being gay and lesbian isn't a lifestyle, although some geniuses chose to apply that label because labels made then comfortable. If you think men and women choose to be gay or lesbian, you should really spend time in the real world. Unfounded conclusions become labels. Labels put people in neat little clusters that we can choose to engage or ignore. If we had made Randy battle hardened, he might have been defensive of his life and might have been more combative and less willing to trust himself to live authentically. Instead, he grew to become a conciliatory young man who saw the good in people and wasn't afraid to be true to himself.

So we know there's no such thing as a civil war, and lesbian and gay are not lifestyle choices. You can choose your shoes but not your life. You can choose to love or choose to hate. Taking the low road and engaging in battle at every turn is a recipe for unhappiness.

Nikki DiCaro

Rolling Stops

"HEY HONEY, HOW WAS YOUR DAY?"

"Fine," he said sounding surly. He could be opaque emotionally. When he as transparent, I knew something was wrong.

"You don't sound fine." He shot me his 'leave it alone' look. I think he knew by now that was a red flag in front of a pissed off bull. "My day wasn't so bad, except for the idiot who thought stop signs didn't apply to her. She was yacking on the mobile phone and acting like the SUV she was driving was the only thing on the road." Hubby mumbled something as he contemplated a thought he wasn't willing to share.

"Did you get into an accident with her?"

"No, but she almost ran down an elderly woman at a crosswalk."

"Ass hat."

"I think she yelled something nasty at the woman; as if she didn't have to yield to her."

"Makes you want to …" His voice trailed off.

"It was the thing I complained about all the time." He started to say something then caught himself. I think he wanted to remind me that I complained about a lot of things.

"It's not what you think. It's about 'rolling stops'."

"Right, people think they're 'stop' with a small 'o'. The lower case 'O' in the word 'stop' means stopping at stop signs is optional." My husband so eloquently explained the concept of the rolling stop. You slow when you approach an intersection, then roll through as if you were the only car on the road. And in your mind, you are!

"Remember when we complained to the police about dangerous intersections?"

"How could I forget." I don't think he was happy to talk about anything we couldn't change.

"Well, Pam was one of the biggest complainers, yet she was the one who was telling everybody who would listen that the police were watching the intersections." Pam was one of the longest residents of our little community and its self-proclaimed Alderman. Or is it Alderwoman. Whatever. I watched my neighbors fail to respect traffic control. I guess they knew better than the experts who placed traffic control devices at strategic places to enable people to cross streets safely. I have this thing about people who think they're more important than a pedestrian and insist on bullying their way around in their several thousand-pound hunk of plastic, aluminum, glass and metal. Motor vehicles are imposing if you're on foot. You don't want to be crushed by someone more important than you. So we step back and catch our breath as the vehicle rumbles by within a hare's breath of sideswiping us. I'm not sure how wide a hare's breath is, but it doesn't sound like it leaves much room for safety.

"Pam warned all the neighbors, who would listen, that the police were watching. She made it a point to undercut exactly what she complained about. Her warning kept people in line and the police stopped watching after three days. Pam was the loudest complainer, then was the one who had the most to say about the police trying to catch people breaking the law."

"She was something else." That was Ralph's way of saying she wasn't anyone he was interested in getting to know.

Have you thought about the ramifications of hitting a pedestrian?

"Officer, I didn't see that person. I think they jumped out in front of my SUV!" The stunned driver claimed. The officer took notes as he prepared to respond.

"You're sure she jumped out in front of your truck."

"It's not a truck, it's an SUV." The driver responded condescendingly.

"You claim this woman jumped?"

"I'm not claiming anything; she did jump. And if she says any different, she's lying!" The driver sounded self-righteous. Paramedics were busy strapping the pedestrian to a rolling gurney. The officer surveyed the activity as several bystanders were recording the event for posterity with their camera phones.

"Ma'am, please step over here."

"Why, am I under arrest?"

"Not yet."

"What do you mean, not yet? I'm calling my husband. He's a lawyer!" She said proudly.

"A criminal lawyer?"

"Uh no, a divorce lawyer." The police officer digested the statement; wondering if the husband would represent himself in a divorce.

"Ma'am, please." The officer directed her with hand signals. The driver looked skeptically as she moved towards the officer. She looked around, trying to absorb what was rapidly becoming distorted reality.

"This is a walker," the officer said, pointing to the mangled tubes of aluminum and plastic. One leg of the walker has a yellow tennis ball attached to the tip. Another tennis ball with a hole in it was lying in the gutter at the cusp of the intersection. The driver's jaw dropped before she composed herself.

"Where did that come from?"

"It belongs to the woman you hit." The officer was beginning to sound like a prosecutor.

"It does not!" The driver's voice and composure began to show signs of cracking.

"Ma'am, this woman couldn't have jumped in front of your truck." The officer pointed to the back of the EMT unit into which the injured pedestrian was being loaded.

"Well I didn't hit her. Maybe she was setting me up." The officer shot her an 'oh yeah, I'm sure that's the way it went down' look.

"I'm going to write a summons for failing to stop at a marked intersection and failing to yield to a pedestrian." He paused for effect. "I'm going to give you a verbal warning about texting while driving. You're lucky she's only injured, although it looks bad." The officer's stare hardened and the driver began to wilt under its intensity.

The officer had seen it before. Distracted driver hits innocent pedestrian and then begins fabricating her version of the truth that she will defend against irrefutable evidence to the contrary.

That's when life takes on a surreal feel. Once well-ordered, one bad decision, one distraction, one preoccupation, one feeling of superiority, and your world becomes a maelstrom. There's no reset button, no rewind and you're not dreaming. Although the situation feels more like a nightmare than a dream. Cutting corners can lead to suboptimal outcomes. That's another way your terd creek without a paddle and insect repellent.

What was once blue skies and sparkling sunshine suddenly turned black and threatening. Thunderclaps of lawsuits and restitution rattle you to the core. You feel remorse, but that won't do. You want to apologize but there are no magic words to unhurt the woman who thought she could safely cross a street. She had faith that you would be awake and aware. She bet you would stop and let her cross safely. People who bet, lose more times than they win. It's the nature of gambling.

Nikki DiCaro

Guessing Games

    Willie works in my office. It's not really my office. It belongs to the owners; I just work there. I do other things so I don't *just* work there. Anyway, Willie Mattres (I pronounce it *Mattress*, he pronounces it *Matters*) likes drama. He enjoys keeping people guessing. I guess that's why he always says 'guess what' before revealing something.
    "Yesterday Frannie walked into the office and, guess what, she told everyone she was pregnant. Some people didn't seem to care, but guess what, Marilyn said Frannie should get married. Frannie looked at Marilyn and guess what, Frannie smiled and said she *was* married."
    Guessing games made my husband apoplectic. Sounds like apocalyptic. I don't think they mean the same thing. The kids, when they were much younger, got into the habit of saying *guess what*.
    "Hey dad, guess what?"
    "I'm not going to guess."
    "Huh? What's daddy talking about *guessing*?"
    "You said "guess what". Daddy thought you wanted him to guess." I tried to be gentle. Ralph wasn't into gentle after he told you something more than once.
    "No. I know daddy hates guessing. That's why he doesn't play some of our board games." Suzanne had her father's number and had no compunction about waving it in his face. My husband listened but tried to appear as if he wasn't paying

attention. The kids had him figured out. Each one picked up on a quirk and seemed to exploit it in ways only kids could pull off.

Willie Mattres, one of my coworker, enjoyed guessing games. He thought he was clever. Willie also would say, "sorta speak" instead of "so to speak". I tried to figure out whether there was a hidden meaning. When I failed, I resorted to asking him. It turned out he thought the phrase was correct. Jarolyn Hobson, another coworker (more like a work sister) refused to cut him slack. She was our self-anointed mother hen – the woman with the institutional knowledge. She was a proud black woman who disdained being labeled a woman of color or African-American. She said everyone had color; some were darker than others. She also stated she was American, born and raised. She didn't need to be identified with a country she had never visited.

"Calling me a woman of color makes it sound like some women have no color." Jarolyn was Mistress Matter-of-Fact. I respected her for being sure of herself. She cut through the fog of bullshit faster than anyone I knew. Even faster than my husband.

Jarolyn and Lovey, her husband (his given name was Frederick) came to dinner a few Sundays. I didn't invite coworkers to my home. I wanted separation between professional and personal. I like Jarolyn so much I considered her a friend. Ralph and I believed you invited friends into your home.

"You've got a beautiful home," Jarolyn said. Lovey and Ralph had already cracked open a couple of beers and were stationed in front of the television. They were two peas in a pod. The better phase would have been two baseballs in a mitt.

"Glad you could get here."

"What is going on with Testosterone dude?" I almost projectile spewed a mouthful of water. I'd never heard her refer to the boss as anything but Mister Wannabe.

"Damn girl, you're gonna make me choke!" I tried to sound offended but it didn't work.

"Well, what do you make of his newest round of nonsense?"

"I think he's insecure or probably lonely."

"Boy's got a funny way of showing it; I'll say that much for him."

"I don't cut him much slack. He thinks I fear him."

"Let him think what he wants honey. You don't owe him anything." I didn't want to discuss work. I tried not to discuss it in the office.

"You think we should feed the boys?"

"Sounds like they're knee deep in the game." She was referring to the color commentary coming from the Family Room. "Let's sit outside and be carefree. When they're hungry, they'll howl." Jarolyn's candidness was a constant reminder my trust was safe in her care.

By the end of the day I was ready for sleep. I enjoyed entertaining, especially seeing friends who hadn't been around for a while. The last time we got together, Jarolyn cooked up what she called her famous blue point special. This was Maryland crabs steamed, cleaned and soaked in a combination of butter, olive oil, cayenne pepper and basil. My lips and fingers felt the heat long after we polished off a couple dozens of those beauties. Lovey finished off the meal by cooking thin spaghetti and coating it with the leftover coating. That meal was creative and one Ralph and I talked about for days afterwards.

You can tell how much a person cares by how much time and effort they invest in a meal. Jarolyn inspired me to take my cooking to the next level; which was probably three levels lower than hers. It's the thought that counts.

Pass the Butter

Recipes:

Chicken Soup ala Amelia

Ingredients:
Half a bulb of fresh garlic – finely chopped
One medium yellow onion – coarsely chopped
Six stalks of celery – coarsely chopped
Four plum tomatoes – sliced (a large can of diced tomatoes can be substituted)
One pound of baby carrots – coarsely chopped or julienned. Packaged carrots already sliced or julienned would be fine.
One baked whole chicken from the supermarket (why cook more than you have to?)
Two quarts' low sodium chicken stock (more stock if you prefer more liquid in your soup)
One half pound lentils, rinsed

Seasonings:
1 tablespoon ground black pepper
1 tablespoon salt
1 teaspoon ground curry
1 teaspoon ground cumin
2-4 tablespoons canola oil

Cooking instructions:
Sautee onions in canola oil. When onions are opaque, add chopped celery and carrots.

Nikki DiCaro

Add chopped garlic when celery softens

Sautee until garlic begins to brown.

Add plum tomatoes and chicken stock and bring to slow boil

Remove skin from the chicken and cut it into large pieces; discarding the back and neck

Bring to a boil before adding lentils

The chicken will eventually fall off the bone. You can remove the bones before serving

Simmer until lentils are tender

Serve with garlic bread and grated Locatelli cheese

Preview the next book in this series: *Pass the Syrup*

How Did I Get Here?

Ever wake up and wonder, how did I get here? I don't mean this physical place. I mean this place, this station in life. Sounds like a train ride, right? *Next station stop adulthood. This is the express to middle age. The next stop will be your thirties! All tickets and passes please.*

I have those thoughts sometimes. Don't get me wrong, I have a good life. Husband, three loving children – well they're not little children anymore.

They'll always by my babies even though they're rapidly approaching teenager. When I woke on a Saturday the house was empty. Looking across the bedroom at the clock radio I blinked twice to clear the sleep from my eyes. I couldn't figure out why we put the clock radio on the deep windowsill across the room. Maybe it was my vision. I can't see close up without reading glasses. Is that near-sighted or far-sighted? It doesn't matter in the scheme of things. Getting out of bed, if I slept past my weekday 6:00 a.m. wake up for work, got harder with each passing year. I'm not ancient but sometimes I feel like an Egyptian artifact.

Ralph took the kids for the day. It's my birthday. Well not today. Actually, my birthday is Monday. We're both working and I told him I didn't want anything big or crazy for the big Three Five. Yep, I'm turning thirty-five years old. Old, the word strikes fear into the heart of women. Women get older, men become more distinguished. Sounds misogynist to me. Distinguished, really? Is that like a distinguishing mark or habit? He farts a lot, that distinguishes him from all the other men my age who fart? Get my drift?

Nobody wants to get old, right? We were just getting used to being young. Somebody said "youth is wasted on the young". I believe that. We should live our lives in reverse. You know, learn all the stuff we learn throughout our lives and have it when we're young. Wouldn't it be amazing to do all the things we become too old or too wary to do before our bodies aren't as supple or don't heal quickly anymore? I think we miss out on so much because we don't have the energy or stamina.

I don't buy the horseshit that we start dying the day we're born. Somebody with a death wish or not enough drugs was feeling particularly sorry for themselves when they wrote those words. We live as long as we allow ourselves to be vibrant and relevant.

Okay, that's the end of the depressing part of the program. Let's move on to my morning. I wandered like a zombie down stairs to the first floor of our four-bedroom suburban home. I'm gonna be thirty-five. I can't shake the thought as I wander into the kitchen for the first jolt of caffeine. There's a post-it note on the coffee maker. We have one of those fancy single cup jobbies. Pop in the measured pod, push the button and coffee comes out. Don't forget to put the cup under the spout; I've done that at least once!

Ralph's a sweetheart. The note says he loves me more than he can say. I wrap myself in my arms, turn three hundred sixty degrees on the balls of my feet and smile. He really does move me even after three kids and all the craziness that comes with raising a family.

The house is quiet except for the gurgling and hissing of the brewer. It's weird. I can't remember the last time the house was quiet. Even when everyone's sleeping, the sound of breathing gives life to the surroundings. Today it's me and the bricks and the furniture ... and my memories. Maybe I'll clean. I don't do cleaning as much anymore. We have a cleaning lady who comes every other week. I clean before she gets here. Sounds nuts, huh? Well we wouldn't want her throwing things out that we need. And we wouldn't want to scare her away by leaving the house in shambles. Anyway, Joyce comes every other Monday. Ralph talked me into hiring her.

"What, our house isn't clean enough for you?" I remember saying as if I thought I needed to defend my responsibility as wife and mother. Ralph blinked. That was the signal he felt like I missed the point. "Are you trying to tell me something?" I felt strange and wasn't sure what I was missing so I shut up for a minute.

Ralph took my hand and led me to the sofa in our large living room with the big bow window dominating the front wall looking out over our sparsely landscaped front lawn and planting beds. We sat next to each other. His eyes were soft, almost apologetic. "I'm sorry Meel (he took to calling me Meel; another pet name he invented). I didn't mean to sound like I was attacking you. Look at me please. I sat for a long moment before turning my gaze away from the cluttered rectangular coffee table.

"What?"

"You're my beautiful wife and the mother of my children." I was trying to figure out where this was going. He was never one for frontal assaults. He was the master of outflanking people emotionally. I felt like he might be going there. "We get two whole days every week to spend together and I can think of better things to do than cleaning. Sure we can do yard work together. I like working next to you. We're good together. But neither of us adds any value to the house cleaning process, right?" His eyebrows rose to punctuate the question.

"And?" I wasn't in the mood for cutting breaks.

"And it's not your job to spend a day cleaning. Would I ever deny you the fun of cleaning? Of course not. Besides, we can afford to hire someone."

"I'm not sure I want somebody going through my underwear drawer." I thought how stupid that must have sounded. Ralph smiled one of his infectious smiles. I joined him. He had me with the smile.

"Really Meel, your underwear drawer? I don't go through your underwear drawer." I pouted through a smile. "I want to go through your underwear while you're wearing them." How did we go from a cleaning lady to my husband undressing me? I wasn't feeling self-conscious. I felt something between sensuality and … well I can't explain the other end of the feeling.

It was time to shift the conversation. "Who are you thinking to clean?" Ralph took my hands in his and then hugged me.

"I checked out a few cleaning services. I asked around at work."

"What?" My voice was shrill, conveying shock. "You talked about cleaning services at work? I don't believe it!" I said pushing back from the embrace.

"Okay, I looked on-line and found four services. I called them and got references. They all sounded good but there was one I liked best." He stood and walked over to the dining room where he kept his backpack. Digging through one of the pockets he extracted a single sheet of paper and handed it to me. I looked it over and thought, *this guy's trying. I need to cut some slack.*

"This is a big deal and I appreciate it. How much is this gonna cost?"

"Trust me, we can afford it. They charge twenty bucks an hour. I'm thinking four hours every week." I calculated the cost and how it would fit into our budget.

"Six hours every two weeks," I countered.

Pass the Butter

"That's okay with me. I want you to be happy."

"Then let's get her to come by the house. We might not like her or she may run away screaming after she sees the place." It was my turn to smile.

"Sold." He pulled me to him and his hands were all over me.

More Works by Nikki DiCaro

If you enjoyed *Pass the Butter*, you can follow Ralph and Amelia and their three children in the other books in this series:

I'm Nobody's Pancake

What, no Bacon?

Pass the Syrup

Top Off My Coffee and Bring the Check

Coming soon:

Chicken Cheese Steak

Sweet Potato Fries

Made in the USA
Middletown, DE
14 January 2024

47385774R00066

THINGS THAT I HAVE SEEN IN GOD!

THINGS THAT I HAVE SEEN IN GOD!

Bishop Nathaniel Gomillion

Gomillion and Gomillion

Prince George, Virginia

Dunamis Publishing Associates

Tuscaloosa, Alabama

2009, Bishop Nathaniel Gomillion, Prince George, VA

All rights reserved under the Pan-American and International Copyright Conventions

Printed in the United States of America

This book may not be reproduced in whole or part, in any form or by any means, electronic or mechanical, including photocopying, recording, or by any information storage and retrieval system now known or hereafter invented, without the permission from the author.

Cover Design: The D J James Group

ISBN: 978-1-60458-511-7

Dunamis Publishing Associates, Inc.

5111 Overbrook Road

Tuscaloosa, Alabama 35405

www.dunamispublishing.com

ACKNOWLEDGEMENTS AND DEDICATION

I thank God for His call upon my life and all of the abilities that He has given me.

I dedicate this second book to my wife, Elder Francine Gomillion. I'm thankful for her unwavering support and prayers.

I, also, dedicate it to my children and my grandchildren. I thank them for believing in and supporting me.

I thank the "TOP" for their support, especially Elder Florence Reynolds for the use of her editing skills.

I also want to thank Bishop Robert E. Williams for teaching me to have confidence in my presentation, Bishop Charles Middleton for inspiring me to publish, the D. James Group for favor and artistic creativity, and Dunamis Publishing Associates for its professionalism.

✝*Bishop Nathaniel Gomillion*

Things That I Have Seen In God

TABLE OF CONTENTS

Foreword	ix
Chapter One – Determination	1
Chapter Two – Maturity	11
Chapter Three – Blooming Late	19
Chapter Four – Faith that really is Faith	27
Chapter Five – Thankfulness	35
Chapter Six – Promises	43
Chapter Seven – Peace	51
Chapter Eight – Moving On	59
Chapter Nine – Resurrection	65
Chapter Ten – Nakedness	71
Chapter Eleven – Beauty	79
Chapter Twelve – Father	91
Chapter Thirteen – Responsibility	99
Chapter Fourteen – Houses	107

Things That I Have Seen In God

FOREWORD

"Things That I've Seen In God" is a masterful piece of simplistic profundity. The ink of inspiration drips from the pen of the evangelist Bishop Nathaniel Gomillion. His approach, in every chapter, bears the marks of the mandate of Calvary. His style of reflective presentation, teaching and preaching engages people according to their philosophical milieu or environment.

These messages may not have the stamp of greatness upon them as many scholars and theologians would count "greatness" in sermonic theory, but to the mature spiritual eye, we can rightly see the stamp of divine inspiration, intervention, and mediation. He has not failed to present Christ and Him crucified.

The Bishop deals with matters that compel us to give attention to the relief of the helpless, hurting, and those hated because of injustices imposed upon them in this world that have resulted in physical and spiritual paralyses.

These messages, once breathed upon by the Holy Spirit and placed in the hand of the reader, will draw hearts and souls to the compassion and grace of Christ.

Prophet Michael Shakespeare
Truth Christian Assembly FGBC, W. Bloomfield, MI

> "PLENTY OF PEOPLE HAVE CRIED OUT TO THE LORD FOR HELP, BUT NOT MANY OF THEM HAVE DONE SO IN WORSHIP AFTER REJECTION."

Chapter One

Determination

Whatever it takes!

Matthew 15:26-27 (KJV) *"**26** But he answered and said, It is not meet to take the children's bread, and to cast it to dogs.*
27 And she said, Truth, Lord: yet the dogs eat of the crumbs which fall from their masters' table."

Things That I Have Seen In God

One of the great realities in life is that much of what we say we *cannot* do is really what we *will not* do. What we say is a lack of ability or opportunity is just a problem of will. Let me use as an example the condition of *that* room in your house. You know *that* room! I'm talking about the one that you say that you didn't have enough time to clean up. In actuality, you don't prioritize the time to clean up *that* room! Don't get defensive! I am not saying that you are wrong to not clean the room. I am saying that you may be "misguided" as to why you are not cleaning it up.

We have some *"that"* areas in our lives. These are areas, like the room, that we say we have the "can't help its." We have concluded that we cannot clean up or make adjustments in those areas of our lives. We have just chosen not to clean up these areas.

One of those areas that we have chosen not to clean up is "attitude." Attitude is defined as a manner of acting, feeling, or thinking that shows one's disposition, opinion, etc. It is a mood, opinion, idea about, viewpoint, standpoint, outlook, perspective, belief, or demeanor. It's how we view people and life in general. Life is about choices and the cost of the adjustments that must be made.

The woman that is referenced in the text was Syrophoenician and as such was considered an outcast to Israel. She was like the little fat kid down the block with buck teeth! She was like the child who stuttered profusely when he talked! She was like the little skinny boy who could not gain weight or who was shorter than all of the other boys his age! She was teased and taunted even though she had nothing to do with her place of birth.

Perhaps you have never been the one teased, but I have. When people are teased by their peers long enough, they tend to develop an ego protective mechanism. It's an attack attitude! Those who persist in pushing the envelope of challenge or overt criticism can become the object of their attacks. From all indications, this woman probably had one of those attitudes. You may have or have had one too!

If we fast forward the tape of her actions, this woman's willingness to deal with her attitude and her willingness to make the proper adjustment could have been the contributing factor to her getting what she needed from the Lord for her daughter. It is evident that there is some stuff that people will not tolerate, until their children are in trouble.

There are some situations that will make you say:

"Whatever I have to be, I will be and whatever level of persistence that I have to exhibit, I will exhibit."

"Whatever price I have to pay, even in losing my dignity, I will pay."

"Whatever it takes, it takes!"

Jesus had finished His teaching on what defiles or makes a man unclean. It was not what went into a man that made him filthy, but what came out of him.

"For out of the heart proceed evil thoughts, murders, adulteries, fornications, thefts, false witness, blasphemies:"

Jesus was approached by this woman with an urgent plea on behalf of her daughter. It is certain that she knew Jesus because she called Him "Messiah" and "Son of David." Her request was for mercy, as she pointed at her daughter, who was possessed with a devil but her pleas were immediately met with rejection on several levels.

The first rejection that she received was from Jesus, Himself. He said nothing. "Nothing" can be the loudest sound that you've ever heard, especially when you are expecting a response. Secondly, the disciples of Jesus, who weren't asked anything by the woman, urged Jesus to send her away. She was not trying to deprive the disciples of anything, but they weighed in on her dilemma, declaring this mother unworthy to ask anything of Jesus based upon her outward appearance. They did not consider her faithfulness but rather her faulty gene pool. She was not a child of Abraham according to the flesh. Don't you hate it when people who do not understand your level of pain weigh in on your dilemma without compassion?

There are two lessons for the disciples and for us to learn: First, we have to learn that no one would approach the Master, calling Him Lord, without some level of faith. Secondly, we must minister from a heart filled with compassion for everybody and not just for those in our little group. We must be prepared to minister to the despised and rejected as well as to the favored and accepted.

When Jesus responded to the woman, after her persistence, He did not send her away as was suggested by the disciples. Neither did He immediately take care of her need. He made a statement of fact:

> "I am not sent but unto the lost sheep of the house of Israel".

> "Then came she and worshipped him, saying, Lord, help me."

After being dismissed earlier and "rejected" later, the mother worshipped Jesus. The word "worship" is from the Greek word "proskuneo," which means to "bow down." It literally means to become prostrate in reverence before God. It is frequently translated "an act of humility." Indeed, that is what this woman did in the face of her circumstances; she threw herself at Jesus' feet.

There are some folks who have never had a worship experience before the Lord. Some actually don't know what it means to worship the Lord and have not sought to experience the joy of it. This mother worshipped the Lord after He had said, "NO" to her request for her daughter. She exhibited a "Whatever it takes worship" and then, persistently said, "Help me!"

Plenty of people have cried out to the Lord for help, but not many of them have done so in worship after rejection. She worshipped the Lord; she kept after Jesus:

- despite His silence,
- despite the objection of the disciples,
- despite her being undeserving,
- despite His rejection.

She worshipped Him and her faithful persistence came out of her worship. He provided her with the spiritual stamina to continue seeking help from Jesus.

The statement that followed the worshipping by this mother has caused much discussion by Bible scholars and those who try to find in language some nuance of translation that is not obvious to the average Bible student.

Things That I Have Seen In God

> *"But he answered and said, 'It is not meet to take the children's bread, and to cast it to dogs.'"*

These words of Jesus appear to have added insult to injury. She had already been rejected and had worshipped Jesus, even after that rejection. On the surface, this could be considered an insult, but, looking deeper, you will discover that the Lord gave this mother a "word to wrestle with." He gave her a word on which to think.

I know what it sounded like:

"You ain't nothing but a lazy...," (You fill in the rest.)

"You ain't ever going to be anything!"

"Boy, you are going to bust hell wide open!"

All, who have taken the important step to accept Jesus as Lord and Savior, have had to make that decision *after* He had given them a "Word to wrestle with." This is usually a "let me show you where your faith needs to go" word! In this particular woman's case, this was a "Let me see how much you really want your daughter healed" word!

The word "dog" was not an offensive phrase. It expressed the fact that Gentiles were "outside" the Covenant privileges of Israel because they were not descendants of Abraham and were, therefore, ineligible to be blessed by God. The mother could have taken this second sign of rejection and walked away. She could have said,

> "Well, that's it. I am not going to take anymore. I'm not going to ask anymore."

That is what pride decorated in ego will do; but pride always manifests itself before its bearer's fall.

There is no doubt that she wrestled with what Jesus said. Do not make the mistake of believing that she did not think about walking away, but every time she thought about walking away, she probably looked at her little girl and said within herself, *"Whatever it takes, it takes!"*

One can only imagine what was going through this mother's mind after what she had experienced. Yet, there was a need that she believed could only be met by Jesus and she was determined not to leave that place of potential deliverance of her daughter from under demonic attack until that need was met.

This mother said (and I'm taking the liberty to paraphrase here): *"This is the Master and if He calls me a dog, then I'll be a dog! All that I need to figure out is what a dog's rights are, because He is a fair God. He would not dare call me 'dog' and then deny me the 'rights' of a dog!"*

She probably demonstrated a spirit of humility that was beyond that of any of the Children of Israel. She did not argue. If dogs got scraps from the table, that would have been enough to at least feed them. The same principle could apply to her daughter, if she only received the "scraps" of blessings from Jesus.

Sometimes, we miss God and miss out on what God could do in our lives by arguing with Him and not being willing to do whatever it takes. We argue over how long we have to worship, how much we should give, or how much prayer is *too* much prayer. We argue over the Lord's sovereignty over our lives. We choose to argue!

This mother understood something that a lot of people do not understand or miss: If Jesus is Lord of all, then, ultimately, He is also Lord of the dogs! If he is responsible for the care of all that He is Lord over, then, ultimately, He is responsible for the care of those, who for whatever reasons, have been rejected.

It was out of her perceived "dogship" that she made a demand on His anointing. She conceded that the perceived problem that her daughter had of being vexed with a devil was just a "crumb problem" in God's sight. The heritage problem - not being kin to Abraham by flesh and the covenant - was a "crumb problem" for Jesus. The same power that was in the loaf was also in the crumbs!

Great was her persistence and her perception of who Jesus was and how He was to operate in her life. Great was her understanding of spiritual things. Her daughter was made whole from that very hour.

"WE HAVE FALLEN IN LOVE WITH WHO WE ARE AND WE HAVE STOPPED TRYING TO BECOME WHAT GOD PUT US HERE TO BECOME."

Chapter Two

Maturity

The Thrill is gone!

1 John 3:2 *"Beloved, now are we the sons of God, and it doth not yet appear what we shall be: but we know that, when he shall appear, we shall be like him; for we shall see him as he is."*

The cited chapter text was penned by John "the beloved disciple" of Christ, who may be seen laying his head on the breast of Christ in most depictions of the Last Supper. He was, reportedly, the last of the disciples to be seen alive on earth. Not only is John the author of this book, but he is also the author of the Gospel of John, which exposes Jesus as God and 2nd John, 3rd John, and the Book of Revelation.

Perhaps you've heard the song, *"The Thrill is Gone,"* by Blues singer, B. B. King, who was also famous for his famous guitar, "Lucille." The lyrics were explicit in expressing his loss of a love relationship, supposedly his wife.

> *"The thrill is gone! The thrill is gone away, Baby..."*

"Thrill" is defined as "excitement." If something is seen as thrilling, it is supposed to be stirring, moving, or rousing. In the song, B. B. King said that the excitement had gone out of his relationship. He was no longer stirred, moved, or aroused in the relationship.

Though this Blues song spoke to a relationship between a man and a woman, it could just as well have spoken to other relationships. It could have referenced the relationships that students have with their schools of learning. It could have application to employee/employer relationships or other examples, where the drudgery of doing the same thing over and over or the pressure of keeping commitments that we've made, make the wine run out.

It is interesting how the wine can run out after we would have started out so on fire. We were determined in our minds to be the best. We were determined to do it all. It did not matter if we had to start early and keep at it until late, we had purposed in our hearts to do be successful. That was the time when the *excitement* of what we were doing made everything seem so easy. Even things that were difficult seemed easy. We were having fun, but then we woke up one day and the thrill was gone.

Many of us started out on fire with God. We wondered why the church doors had to ever be closed. We were there when the doors opened. We just wanted to be in God's presence. We wanted more of God. We wanted to be a "Christian" like the world had never seen. If we had an evil passing thought in our hearts, it grieved us immensely. We desired to desperately grow in grace, but, now, the thrill is gone!

As a result, we have settled for "just good enough." We have fallen in love with who we are and we have stopped trying to become what God put us here to become. "The enemy of best can be better, just like the enemy of better can be good."[1] You can be destined for higher ground and fall in love with middle ground. You, on the other hand, may become overly glad that you are not on low ground and forget that there are still mountains to climb.

You should be speaking in tongues and laying hands on the sick and casting out devils, but you are satisfied with just being saved.

> *"Beloved, now are we the sons of God, and it doth not yet appear what we shall be: but we know that, when He shall appear, we shall be like Him; for we shall see Him as He is."*

We are the offspring of God. We have been born again. Everyone who exercises genuine saving faith becomes a child of God at the moment of his belief. John 1:12-13 records:

> *"But as many as received him, to them gave He power to become the sons of God, even to them that believe on his name: 13 Which were born, not of blood, nor of the will of the flesh, nor of the will of man, but of God."*

Paul says in Romans 8:16:

> *"The Spirit itself beareth witness with our spirit, that we are the children of God".*

We are already saved though the divine life in us will not be revealed until Jesus appears.

---

[1] Voltaire [François Marie Arouet] (1694–1778), French philosopher, author. "Dramatic Art," Philosophical Dictionary (1764)

Meanwhile, the Holy Spirit is working in us to conform us into the image of Christ. He is working in us, but He needs our cooperation. We must desire to be conformed to that image.

Each time we put something to print, we examine existing commentary on texts which may have variable interpretations. One commentator has noted that there may be a tension between the first part of the verse *("...now we are children")* and the latter part ("*...we shall be like Him"*).

If there is "tension" in the text, it is between our beginning state in God, where we are children of God by faith, but look nothing like God, and the statement of what we can become and what we will look like in our latter state. The tension may only be resolved by keeping the hope alive of becoming what the text says we *can* become. It comes from reviving the thrill that may be gone or by replacing the wine that has run out of our relationship with God.

I like the word "now" because it stipulates we *are* already the children of God. We are saved by grace. We are His children, even when we don't look anything like Him. We are His children though we know little about whom He is or what He would have us to do to glorify Him. Though we lack the power to flow like He wants us to flow, we are still His children.

We have been adopted (past tense) into the family of God. The moment that you have faith in Christ, salvation is in effect. The moment that we accept His atoning sacrifice on Calvary is the basis of our acceptance by God. The moment that we can sing with faith:

> *"At the cross, at the cross where I first saw the light and the burdens of my heart rolled away, it was there by faith, I received my sight and now I am happy all the day."*[2]

It is at that moment we can change the tense of the text and make it personal: *"Now I am a child of God."*

We are excited to be saved and to have escaped hell, but we may not understand the cost of the grace that has been applied to our lives!

God's grace is appreciated by our efforts. There is a spiritual maturity that must become apparent in our lives. We shall become something that we are not yet. We can be more than what we are. The question is *how* do we make what we can become appear?

The short answer is "faith." The Book of James says: **"Faith without works is dead."**

---

[2] At The Cross Words by Isaac Watts, Music by Charles H. Gabriel, 1905

There is no such thing as faith that is not involved in the activity of being faithful. If I believe that there is something that I *can* be and that something does not appear, then I should be doing all that I can to make it appear. An appropriate appreciation of what it cost God to apply grace to my life and give me an expected end requires that I be faithful. It requires that I work to get to that expected end. It requires that I be willing to pay the cost of the effort *to become*.

Maturity is marked by glory, seen in the life of a Believer. Glorification is the final stage of a Christian's life. When we read: **"We shall be changed in a moment, in the twinkling of an eye,"** we are reading about glorification.

Before there is final change, there are "changes" that lead *to* the final change. It starts with changes in our choices, as when we move from deciding to make Jesus our choice to making Jesus' choices in our lives. It is when we decide that after we get the answer to what Jesus would do, that we actually do it. We must have a desire to go on into spiritual maturity, to get the thrill back in our relationships. We need to get the wine back in.

"WE CAN FAIL AT DOING A THING FOR YEARS AND, BECAUSE OF PROPHETIC UTTERANCE, SUCCEED AT WHAT WE HAD PREVIOUSLY FAILED."

Chapter Three

Blooming Late

Better Late than Never

Luke 1:13 (KJV) "*But the angel said unto him, Fear not, Zacharias: for thy prayer is heard; and thy wife Elisabeth shall bear thee a son, and thou shalt call his name John.*"

Things That I Have Seen In God

All of us have heard the statement: "It's better late than never." It is a statement that may have been used toward someone who had possibly chided us about our tardiness. It suggests that it is better to have done something late than not to have done it at all.

The statement could describe someone who spent his life struggling to succeed and, seemingly, could not make it, but, late in his life, God blessed him to bloom.

We could have uttered the same statement about someone whom we knew "made it into the kingdom on their last breath. " It could have been someone who spent his entire life, like the thief on the cross, messing up and on their last leg accepted Christ.

We could call these persons "late bloomers." Late bloomers are flowers that appear as though they would never bloom, but seem to find a little more season of blooming, when it a appears the blooming season is long past.

This text is about two late bloomers: Zacharias and Elizabeth. They were both righteous before God, walking in all the commandments and ordinances of the Lord without blame. Zacharias was a priest of the order of Abia, the eighth of the twenty-four courses into which priests had been originally divided by David. His wife was also born of a priestly family.

Things That I Have Seen In God

The priests served at the temple twice each year for a week. Zacharias' time had come for this service and his home was one of the chambers set aside for the priests on the temple grounds.

The offering of incense was one of the most solemn parts of the daily worship of the temple and lots were daily drawn to determine who should have this great honor, which no priest could expect to have more than once during his lifetime.

Elizabeth was a barren woman, living in a world where "female credibility" was afforded based upon child birth. Not only did she have to have birthed a child to be seen as "blessed," but she had to bear at least one male child. Fertility was viewed as a blessing and barrenness was seen as a curse. It is often the case that the customs make the Word of God of little effect and are weighted far beyond that which God has to say about an issue. We place emphasis on areas in which God does not and put people in bondage that need not be there. This had to have caused the couple some level of pain.

Can you imagine loving God, as they did, and having it look like God did not love you? He interceded on behalf of others, who had already received what they repeatedly petitioned God to receive, and yet it appeared that God had not heard his prayers.

If he was a priest by thirty and past child-producing age, he had been praying for a long time. He had been ringing heaven on his bosom cell, with no response from God - no results. It was as though God had not heard him.

He probably tried to avoid situations where his pain or his perceived inadequacies would be noticed by those around him. He had no successor to his name or to his position as priest. It seemed like every time he turned around, someone was bringing up what his "little Ezekiel" or "Esther" was doing.

Has anybody ever been there? You are a preacher, deacon, trustee, choir member, saint of God, who always replies to, "How are you doing?" with "I'm blessed." Yet, you are barren in the area of your life where you want to produce the most: barren finances, barren educational opportunities, barren faith, barren prosperity for your children, barren social success, etc. There is something that you wished nobody would bring up and, yet, it's the one thing that always comes up in every conversation.

- ✓ The school their child graduated from.
- ✓ The successful marriage that they have.
- ✓ Their new house.
- ✓ The new job making more cash than they need.

It is not as though you have not been praying about it, it just seems like your prayers have been futile. You have been faithful in your part, but your circumstances make you look unfaithful.

That was probably the plight of Zacharias. He looked at his life, his perceived lack of longevity, his wife's pain, and possibly doubted everything that he had ever heard about God. At the same time, he was not only to worship himself, but to lead others in worship. He had to offer sacrifices on behalf of himself and on behalf of the people. He had to get himself so much together that he could execute the functions of his office flawlessly. If he had gone into that temple and God had found anything wrong in him, he would not have walked out but would have been dragged out. He had to find faith in what looked like a failed situation.

The lot fell on him, according to God's divine timing, and he was assigned to offer sacrifices at the golden altar. God has his destiny well in hand. While Zacharias ministered at the golden altar of incense in the holy place, God interrupted his worship with an announcement that was sent via the angel, Gabriel.

I submit to you that there are several factors for Zacharias being a late bloomer: The first is "answered prayer." The opening statement from Gabriel was:

"Fear not. Thy prayer is heard." I do not believe that this prayer was one that he prayed yesterday or even recently. I don't believe that he had prayed this particular prayer in a while, but God heard him whenever he prayed about this matter.

I certainly am not suggesting that we should not continue to pray and keep our petitions before God; I am pointing out, however, that God remembered the prayer that Zacharias thought God had forgotten. His blooming late was neither his persistent prayer efforts nor his unwavering faith, but the integrity of God's hearing.

> **"We know that if God hears us we have the petitions that we ask."**

Secondly, Gabriel prophesied: "Thy wife, Elisabeth, shall bear thee a son." This child was to come from the two of them. The angel said that God was going to make them physically able to produce what they, heretofore, could not produce. We can fail at doing a thing for years and, because of prophetic utterance, succeed at what we had previously failed. The word that the angel spoke into the life of Zacharias and Elizabeth was a clear indication that what had not been working in his life was about to start working. Not only was it going to work, but it was going to work in a big way!

Finally, the angel prophesied: *"Thou shalt call his name John."* This late blooming for this couple was about the *glory* that God was going to receive. What

God is going to do is not only about you but it is about God! Miracles are more about the *miracle worker* than about the one experiencing the miracle.

God promised them a son that would not bear the name *of* his father, but a name *for* God. It had been the custom that a man-child was named after someone in the family, but there was nobody in the family named "John."

Not only was the name given, but the purpose for his coming was delineated in Luke 1:15 – 17:

> *"For he shall be great in the sight of the Lord, and shall drink neither wine nor strong drink; and he shall be filled with the Holy Ghost, even from his mother's womb.*
> *16 And many of the children of Israel shall he turn to the Lord their God.*
> *17 And he shall go before him in the spirit and power of Elias, to turn the hearts of the fathers to the children, and the disobedient to the wisdom of the just; to make ready a people prepared for the Lord."*

John was not only the result of "answered prayer" and "after prime production," but he was the result of "accurate prophecy" that Zacharias did not know included him.

God has included each of us in Bible prophecy. As John was the forerunner for Jesus' incarnation, we are the forerunners of His Second Coming. He is coming back again. I believe that, through the process of spiritual maturity, glorification can and will cause us to bloom in the here and now!

Chapter Four

Faith that really is Faith!

IF!!

Mark 9:23 (KJV)
23 Jesus said unto him, If thou canst believe, all things are possible to him that believeth.

24 And straightway the father of the child cried out, and said with tears, Lord, I believe; help thou mine unbelief.

"If" is a two letter word, but it has several meanings. It is also a word that impacts our English and faith tremendously. Consider some of the "ifs" in the Bible:

Genesis 4:7 (KJV)
7 If thou doest well, shalt thou not be accepted? and if thou doest not well, sin lieth at the door. And unto thee shall be his desire, and thou shalt rule over him.

Joshua 24:15 (KJV)
15 And if it seem evil unto you to serve the LORD, choose you this day whom ye will serve; whether the gods which your fathers served that were on the other side of the flood, or the gods of the Amorites, in whose land ye dwell: but as for me and my house, we will serve the LORD.

Psalm 130:3 (KJV)
3 If thou, LORD, shouldest mark iniquities, O Lord, who shall stand?

Psalm 139:8 (KJV)
8 If I ascend up into heaven, thou art there: if I make my bed in hell, behold, thou art there.

Isaiah 1:19-20 (KJV)
19 If ye be willing and obedient, ye shall eat the good of the land:
20 But if ye refuse and rebel, ye shall be devoured with the sword: for the mouth of the LORD hath spoken it.

Matthew 6:14-15 (KJV)
14 For if ye forgive men their trespasses, your heavenly Father will also forgive you:
15 But if ye forgive not men their trespasses, neither will your Father forgive your trespasses.

Things That I Have Seen In God

Romans 10:9 (KJV)
9 That if thou shalt confess with thy mouth the Lord Jesus, and shalt believe in thine heart that God hath raised him from the dead, thou shalt be saved.

Romans 8:31 (KJV)
31 What shall we then say to these things? If God be for us, who can be against us?

There are 1,602 "ifs" in the Bible and our text is about "If!"

Jesus had just been transfigured on the mountain with Moses and Elijah. He had come to that place with Peter, James, and John, where they would spend some time with God. Peter wanted to build three tabernacles and lodge there for a while. God interrupted his plans with the words, *"This is my beloved son, hear Him!"* God dispensed some revelatory truth about the preeminence of His Son.

While they were basking in the presence of God, Satan was taking occasion to come against them with those who were *not* chosen for this level of revelation and who were still at the base of the mountain. Satan will never come against us while we are in the presence of God.

Jesus came down to find the other disciples engulfed by what the Bible described as a "great multitude" and being questioned by some scribes. A man in the crowd spoke to Jesus, saying:

> *"Master, I have brought unto thee my son, which hath a dumb spirit; 18 And wheresoever he taketh him, he teareth him: and he foameth, and gnasheth with his teeth, and pineth away: and I spake to thy disciples that they should cast him out; and they could not".*

The man brought his son to the Omnipotent One and when he saw him (I believe that this he is the demon that chose to demonstrate), the Bible says, *"straightway the spirit tare him; and he fell on the ground, and wallowed foaming".*

The Master inquired of this distraught and loving father:

> *"How long is it ago since this came unto him? And he said, Of a child.*
> *22 And ofttimes it hath cast him into the fire, and into the waters, to destroy him: but if thou canst do anything, have compassion on us, and help us".*

This man linked his son's plight to his own by saying, *"Help us."* The father, also, because of the apparent impotence of the Lord's disciples in handling the matter, had doubts about whether the *teacher* of these disciples had any more power to respond to this honest request. That is why he said, *"If thou canst do anything?"*

Let's not beat up on this man too quickly, because all of us have some "if thou can do anything" in us, periodically. All of us have some things that are dysfunctional. The boy had been dysfunctional since he was child; some of our struggles have been with us a long time. These may be family members, areas of our character, areas of our physical well-being, or spiritual areas.

We may have taken some things to the Lord or to His representatives and been disappointed about their *weak,* anemic, or lack of responses. Speaking outside of the Spirit may cause us to make statements out of the flesh. "*If* you can do anything…"

The response of Jesus was equally challenging to the man:

> **"If thou canst believe, all things are possible to him that believeth."**

First, "possibility" is not the issue. It deals with potential. Possibility is a state of being possible or capable of existing, happening, or being done. If we closely examine this exchange, we can see that, while the man inquired "if" Jesus could do anything, the response of Jesus was that there exist the possibility that He could do everything!

> Luke 1:37, **"For with God nothing shall be impossible".**

When we are dealing with situations that look impossible, we need a "possible!"

It may be deliverance.

It may be a loan.

It may be healing.

It could be a number of things on an exhaustive list of needs. Whatever it is or no matter how hopeless it may appear, it is possible.

Secondly, the reality of possibility is an "If – proposition" - a proposal that can be accepted or rejected. There are business propositions, personal propositions, and some *very* personal propositions. The proposition that Jesus offered this father and that He offers us is that "all things are possible. The proposal to the man is that his son's deliverance from this long term affliction was possible. It was possible for this man's son to stop demonstrating the schizoid behavior of throwing himself in the fire one time and the water the next.

That which was *possible* to happen was *conditional* and would only happen if the man met the conditions of the proposition. This proposition depended on the word "if." The positive possible outcome would only manifest itself, if the man could believe.

This is what stands in the way of us getting our business fixed. It is not the impossibility of a fixing, but our unbelief in the fixing. It's about the "if." Possibility will only become reality if we remove unbelief.

A lot of what we have said about *God*'s denying us may have really been about our denying ourselves. We deny ourselves by not being willing to deal with that which stands in the way of our deliverance.

It is the same as what Jesus said to Mary and Martha: *"Take away the stone."* Take away that which is standing between you and what can be "resurrected." Before we can and will take away the stone, we must admit that it is there!

This man did and cried out with tears,

"Lord, I believe; help thou mine unbelief."

His stone was an admission that he had something in him that was in the way. He had something in him that was standing in the way between what was prophetically possible and what could become his reality. That something was "unbelief."

The man asked for help in destroying that which was trying to destroy him. Unbelief will destroy us. It will cause those of us who have privilege to be healed, to live *beneath* our privilege. Unbelief will cause those who have privilege to live as "more than conquerors" to live conquered lives. Like a little leaven or yeast will mess up the whole lump, it only takes a little unbelief to destroy your destiny.

When this man said, ***"Lord I believe, help my unbelief"***, he was simply asking the Lord to take this demonic "if" out of his life.

Chapter Five

Thankfulness

IT'S NOT 4TH THURSDAY!

Col 1:12 - Col 1:19 (KJV)

Giving thanks unto the Father, which hath made us meet to be partakers of the inheritance of the saints in light: 13 Who hath delivered us from the power of darkness, and hath translated us into the kingdom of his dear Son:

Things That I Have Seen In God

There are many personal and group behaviors that are associated with different dates on the calendar. At Christmas, there is more liberality in giving. People will stop to open the door for people and help carry packages. However, the abundance of kindness seems to disappear as the Christmas Season wanes.

New Year is the time to be optimistic and positive, however, after New Year's Day, pessimism sets in and it's back to "I'm just trying to make it." Valentine's Day suggests that it is all right to openly and unashamedly love someone without being called a "wimp." You may go back to "wimp status" the next day, but on Valentine's Day, you're good to go!

What about the 4th Thursday in November? You know the day; it is the last holiday before Christmas. It is the day before "Black Friday," when all of the retailers hope to make most of their profits for the year. It's the time when most of us show appreciation for all God has done. It is Thanksgiving!

Though these behaviors: kindness, optimism, love, and thankfulness are abundantly displayed during their particular seasons, they are often only displayed for reputation sake. Character may have nothing to do with it. These behaviors are often displayed because it is the "right thing" to do in that season. It is politically correct and publicly expected! Our reputations may be at stake if we don't display the proper behavior at the proper time.

Good character dictates that if the characteristic is good and ordained by God to be done, we must do it in season and out of season. We may not have a ham or turkey at the house with the stuffing on the side or the giblet gravy, hot rolls, and cranberry sauce in the refrigerator, but, yet, we can still give thanks. It may not be the 4th Thursday in November, but it should still be Thanksgiving.

Everyday should be Thanksgiving for the Child of God. Our Thanksgiving should not be based upon a date on the calendar, but on a disposition in our hearts. Our thanksgiving is not something that has to be *pumped* out of us. We should awaken with thanksgiving in our hearts and in our mouths.

There should be daily contemplation on Jehovah and all that He has done for us, creating a worshipful spirit in us. A heart that overflows with praise and is overjoyed about all that the Lord has done should explode in to a crescendo of worship as we enter His house with thanksgiving and enter His courts with praise.

No drum should pound harder than our heart and no trumpet should sound louder that our voice and no harp should make a sweeter melody than the one that comes out of us as we offer up thanksgiving to God! God's love that has been on display by His care for us should cause our souls to long after Him just as the deer pants for the water brook.

The apostle Paul has made it very clear that anybody who is faithful in his assignment as a saint will be the target of attack by the enemy. All who will live Godly shall suffer persecution. They will be under attack, externally, from Satan and internally from their own flesh. When they would do good, evil would be present in them. When a saint struggles with inner *and* outer demons, he cannot subdue them on his own; yet, grace is sufficient.

A believer has to grow in grace. We all have to grow in our understanding of grace and our application of grace. A believer should be able to walk worthy, be fruitful in everything, increase in knowledge of God, and be empowered by Him. This should result in having supernatural patience for the short term trials, longsuffering for the long term trials that will not go away, and the ability to remain joyous through whatever he has to go through.

One commentator said that Paul's prayer was a model or pattern for all Believers to follow. This is consistent with all of the prayers that he offered in his letters to the various churches. To the Philippians Paul wrote:

> *"Be anxious for nothing, but in everything by prayer and supplication with thanksgiving let your requests be made known to God."*

1 Timothy 2:1

> *"entreaties and prayers, petitions and thanksgivings, be made on behalf of all men."*

Colossians 4:2

> *"devote yourselves to prayer, keeping alert in it with an attitude of thanksgiving."*

Giving thanks should never be demoted to a secondary behavior for a child of God. Thanksgiving should be the main thing. It is commanded: *"O give thanks unto the Lord; be thankful unto Him and bless His holy Name."*

Because of our past experiences with God, we have so much to be thankful for. We can be thankful for life, strength, health, welfare, and a number of benefits that have been provided as a bi-product of our serving the Master. These are the creature comforts that God gives us that have nothing to do with our salvation. God kept us until we came to our senses and accepted Him as our keeper, Lord, and Savior, the Christ.

He qualifies us.

The Father made us fit or adequate to be partakers. He has made us fit or adequate for a portion of the inheritance. It is for our allotted portion or inheritance that is situated in the Kingdom of Light. Dakes'

Commentary says that this refers to every promise and every provision of the gospel for believers.

He causes us to quit.

God has qualified us for an inheritance that we will never be able to enjoy without being able to quit the Kingdom of Darkness. It is the kingdom that all of us who were born of the DNA of Adam were born into.

We did not have to "become" sinners; we came into this world with the sin nature. We came here with a natural proclivity for dark things. We were trapped in that kingdom until God made a way for us to escape.

God made a way for us to say, "I quit." "I quit," even if I cannot quit *all* of the behavior that is associated with *where* I am quitting.

God rescued us from (ek) the power (exousias) of the kingdom of darkness (skotous) in which we were held as slaves.

God helped us when we had no power to quit *what* we may have wanted to quit. Deliverance is not the only thing to be thankful for, but every day that we wake up, and we are still free, we ought to be thankful.

He equips us.

Paul used the Greek word "Methistēmi" or (transferred) which means to remove or change. It is used to speak of God's removing Saul from being king or the displacement of a conquered people to another land. The verb speaks here of our total removal from the domain of satanic darkness to the glorious light of the kingdom of Christ. God has changed our address from the kingdom of darkness to the kingdom of light.

We have been placed under the government of the Son of God. God equips us with a born again experience that we could not provide for ourselves - an experience without which we could not enjoy the Kingdom for which He has already qualified us. You already know that you cannot put new wine in old bottles.

We have been redeemed through His blood, which means that our sins have been forgiven. This is the blood of He who is the image of the invisible God, the firstborn of every creature:

> *"All things were created by Him, that are in heaven, and that are in earth, visible and invisible, whether they be thrones, or dominions, or principalities, or powers: all things were created by Him, and for Him."*

When we understand what God has done for

Things That I Have Seen In God

us and how He did it, we cannot help but to be thankful.

Every time that I think about the cross, I think about how messed up I was and where He brought me from. Joy bells start ringing in my soul.

Chapter Six

Promises

I Promise You! - He Promised..,

Psalm 9:9-10 (KJV)
9 The LORD also will be a refuge for the oppressed, a refuge in times of trouble.
10 And they that know thy name will put their trust in thee: for thou, LORD, hast not forsaken them that seek thee.

Most of us are familiar with promises. We have been hearing them all of our lives. They started when we were children, even though the word "promise" was not stated.

Let me see if I can make this real. "If you get good grades in school, I will take you to Disney World." That is a promise without the word "promise" being mentioned. There are many of these types of promises which include: "Will you marry me?" That is also a promise that does not mention the word "promise." Then there are the notes that we sign--mortgages, credit card applications, etc. These, too, are promises without the word promise being mentioned.

Then there are promises like, "I promise to give it to you on Friday"! One of the newest colloquial slang statements is "I promise you"! "Child, he did it right in front of everybody—I promise you." This is a statement that is meant to assure the one that is being told something that the speaker is telling the absolute truth.

What is a promise anyway? A promise is defined as an assurance that one will or will not undertake a certain action or behavior. Promises are either believed or disbelieved, and they are believed or disbelieved based upon a number of things. At the top of the list are those things that would cause us to believe or disbelieve is the one who is making the promise. The person making the promise may cause

Things That I Have Seen In God

the one being promised to ask, *"Does this person have the resources to accomplish what he or she has said that they will do."* The other thing that a person who is receiving a promise might ask himself is whether this person has the integrity to deliver on what he has promised.

Promises that are not taken seriously by the beneficiary are not taken seriously because they do not believe that the person promising is serious about the promise.

If I were asked to rename the Bible, I would rename it the "Promised Land" book. I would rename it that because it really is the land that the promises are in.

Just consider some of the promises that are in this Book, "On the day that you eat you will surely die". That is a negative promise that Adam and Eve did not believe, but there are others that are positive. Some even contain positives *and* negatives. Consider Genesis 12:1-3:

> [1]*"Now the Lord had said unto Abram, Get thee out of thy country, and from thy kindred, and from thy father's house, unto a land that I will shew thee:* [2]*And I will make of thee a great nation, and I will bless thee, and make thy name great; and thou shalt be a blessing:* [3] *And I will bless them that bless thee, and curse him that curseth thee: and in thee shall all families of the*

earth be blessed".

How about Isaiah 1:19-20?

> *"If ye be willing and obedient, ye shall eat the good of the land:*
> *[20] But if ye refuse and rebel, ye shall be devoured with the sword: for the mouth of the LORD hath spoken it."*

Can I give you several more?

II Corinthians 5:1 records:

> *"For we know that if our earthly house of this tabernacle were dissolved, we have a building of God, a house not made with hands, eternal in the heavens."*

John 14:1-3 says:

> *"Let not your heart be troubled: ye believe in God, believe also in me. [2]"In my Father's house are many mansions: if it were not so, I would have told you. I go to prepare a place for you. [3]And if I go and prepare a place for you, I will come again, and receive you unto myself; that where I am, there ye may be also."*

I do not know about you, but I am glad for the promises of God because they give me something for which I can hope. His Promises give all believers hope because hoping is one of the prime functions of the faithful.

It is because we believe the Father that we can join the psalmist in saying, "The Lord is my shepherd and I shall not want". We know the psalmist. He is like one of our family members.

Things That I Have Seen In God

His story is a story with which each of us can identify. David was born into a family that was not royalty and yet he became royalty. David, himself, was the "least" of all of his brothers and by God's grace he catapulted over all of them to become their leader. David contained courage in his being that was not indicative of his size or lack of experience. His courage was beyond his stature.

Though we would not like to have David's family problems, there is in most of us the desire to be like David. Tell me that you would not like to come from nowhere to being on top of everything. Tell me that you would not like to possess the gates of your enemies.

David experienced the reality of all that God had promised and he was uniquely qualified to tell us and to teach us about promises. Within this particular Psalm, David centered his thoughts on the theme of God's consistency in meeting the needs of His people.

The Life Application Bible notes tell us that the basic theme of this Psalm is that God never ignores our cries for help. If you need backup on that, we have to look no further than I John 5:14-15:

> *[14]"This is the confidence we have in approaching God: that if we ask anything according to His will, He hears us. [15]And if we know that He hears us—whatever we*

ask—*we know that we have what we asked of Him"*.

In the first verse of the Psalm, David acknowledges God's extraordinary interventions on behalf of His people. He says in verse two that he would be glad to rejoice in God and to praise His name! Can you look back over your life and see instances when God brought you out? I am talking about when you could've sung, *"Never could have made it without you."*

Consider the words of David in verses 3 – 10:

"When mine enemies are turned back, they shall fall and perish at that presence. ⁴For thou hast maintained my right and my cause; thou satest on the throne judging right. ⁵Thou has rebuked the heathen, thou hast destroyed the wicked, thou hast put out their name for ever and ever. ⁶O thou enemy, destructions are come to a perpetual end: and thou has destroyed cities; their memorial is perished with them. ⁷ But he Lord shall endure forever; He hath prepared His throne for judgment. ⁸ And He shall judge the world in righteousness; He shall minister judgment to the people in uprightness. ⁹The Lord also will be a refuge for the oppressed, a refuge in times of trouble. ¹⁰ And they that know thy name will put their trust in thee: for thou, Lord hast not forsaken them that seek thee."

- God is a hiding place.

    o Vs 9 "The LORD also will be a refuge for the oppressed, a refuge in times of trouble."*

- God can be trusted.

Things That I Have Seen In God

- o Vs. 10a "And they that know thy name will put their trust in thee."*

• God has a track record.

- o Vs.10b "For thou, LORD, hast not forsaken them that seek thee."*

God will never forsake those who seek Him. To forsake someone is to abandon that person. God's promise does not mean that if we trust in Him we will escape loss or suffering; it means God Himself will never leave us no matter what we face.

*<u>Life Application Study Bible.</u>

"TOO OFTEN, THERE IS GREAT SPIRITUAL UNREST IN THOSE WHO ARE SUPPOSED TO BE CONNECTED TO THE CHRIST."

Chapter Seven

Peace

This is the Place!!

Mat 11:28 (KJV)

Come unto me, all ye that labour and are heavy laden, and I will give you rest.

The word "place" is defined as a city, a town, or a village. A "place" can be a residence or dwelling. It can also be defined as rank or status. Our home is a place. Our church is a place. Even our worksite is a place.

We pretty well know about our place in society: middle class, upper class or, well, the other class. We all know what "a place" is and what "our place" is, but what about "the place?"

In my young "rattle snake days," there was always a place that was called "the place." They had "the place" in St. Louis. They had "the place" in Augusta, GA. They had "the place" in Fayetteville, NC. They had "the place" in the Petersburg area, and in every other city that I have ever lived in or been in. (Walkers Green Door, The Mouse Trap, U knows, or the third house on the left hand side of the street where they serve their stuff in jelly jars and you can get your hit in the back room.)

You may not know where "the place" is, but all you have to do is ask anybody in the know and they can tell you where "the place" is. Gamblers know where the bookie is and sexual adventurers know where the blue light district is.

My wife can tell you where to get this or get that on sale and she can tell you about "the place." In the church world, you can go to any city and ask any saint that has been a saint in that city for a while where "the place" is and they can tell you where the "hot place" to worship is located. They can tell you where "the place" is with the hot choir or where "the place" is with the "squalling preacher."

It's very interesting, however, many of these same church folks can tell you where "the place" to worship is but they can't tell you where the place is to find rest. They cannot tell you, because many of them are in so much spiritual unrest themselves. Too often, there is great spiritual unrest in those who are supposed to be connected to the Christ.

There can be those who seem to be *in* place, but they are yet *out* of place. In the cited text, Jesus dealt with such a crowd. Jesus had just finished dealing with a matter of unbelief in his cousin, John. Isn't it amazing how you can find unbelief in the place that you would least suspect it?

John had been jailed for preaching the truth about King Herod's marrying his brother's wife. John also watched many of his faithful followers leave his camp and join themselves to Jesus. John; therefore, sent his disciples to inquire whether Jesus was indeed, the Messiah.

The irony in that inquiry was that this is the same Jesus of whom John had previously testified,

> *"Behold the Lamb of God which taketh away the sins of the world."*

This is the same Jesus that John had baptized, saw the Holy Spirit descending upon him in the form of a dove, and heard God say:

> *"This is my beloved Son in whom I am well pleased."*

Jesus answered John and encouraged him in his crisis, but He did not give up on him.

> *"Verily I say unto you, Among them that are born of women there hath not risen a greater than John the Baptist: notwithstanding he that is least in the kingdom of heaven is greater than he.*

From here, Jesus turned His attention to the Jewish brethren who had rejected both John and Jesus. Jesus denounced the cities in which most of his miracles had been performed because they did not repent.

Jesus' pointed denouncements seemed hard, but, remember, Jesus used this tone because the people of those cities did not repent and were religious people. These people thought that they had it going on! These people thought that they knew "the place" to find rest in Abraham. They had been heard to brag:

> *"We be Abraham's seed."*

In many ways, their bragging was similar to our bragging about being "Baptist," "Holiness," "Methodist," "Apostolic," or "Full Gospel."

Jesus addressed people who were conceited, but who did not know that they were conceited.

> *"Come unto me, all ye that labor and are heavy laden, and I will give you rest."*

This was a formal order as well as an invitation to those whom he had just finished rebuking. It was an invitation to those who were hung up in a religious system that did not and could not provide what they needed. This was an invitation for them to become citizens in the Kingdom of God.

The second thing that the text contains is the conditions under which they could accept the invitation. The command, "Come unto me" was not for everybody. It was not for that group that was wise in their own conceits. It was for those who knew that they were heavy laden and burdened down. To be laden is to be loaded, but this was not for people who were just "loaded," but for those who were heavily loaded. What they were carrying had become an obstacle to them.

The implication is that the one who is invited must recognize for himself that they are heavy laden and burdened down. The Lord already knows that we are, but our free moral agency requires that we come into that knowledge and then make the decision to come to the only one Who can cure us.

Have you ever watched someone struggle with something that they thought that they could carry? They knew that it was too heavy for them, but they thought that they could carry it anyway. You may have tried to help them, but they refused to accept help repeatedly. When we realize that we are heavy laden and burdened down with stuff that we don't have to carry, come to Jesus.

The final facet of the text is *Correction*. Jesus said,

"I will give you rest."

Can I tell you what Jesus does? He applied the word "rest" to Himself. He said that He is rest.

> *"If you come to me, I will give you Myself. I will give Myself for you so that you can have rest. I will provide the sacrifice that will enable you to stop wrestling with your sin."*

Jesus will give you the peace that dead religion cannot give you. He will give you a refreshing spirit. If you follow Christ, you will find refreshment in your renewed relationship with him. You will find freedom from guilt over sin, deliverance from fear and despair, and the promise of continued help and guidance from the Holy Spirit.

Things That I Have Seen In God

To put it simply, Jesus said, "I am 'the Place.'"

> *"Take my yoke upon you, and learn of me; for I am meek and lowly in heart: and ye shall find rest unto your souls. 30 For my yoke is easy, and my burden is light."*

I do not care what type of religious demon that you have been struggling with or how long you have been struggling; there is a place in God for you.

God told Moses, *"There is a place by me."*

I am convinced that "the place" is Jesus and He can provide rest for your weary soul. He can do for you what no other power on earth can do.

"ONE OF THE REASONS FOR SO MUCH BROKENNESS AMONG THE PEOPLE OF GOD IS THAT WE DON'T PLACE A PRIORITY ON HEARING THE WORD OF GOD."

Chapter Eight

Moving On

How to get pass it!

Nehemiah 8:10 (KJV) **Then he said unto them, Go your way, eat the fat, and drink the sweet, and send portions unto them for whom nothing is prepared: for this day is holy unto our Lord: neither be ye sorry; for the joy of the LORD is your strength.**

This is a story about a release from a burden. This is not a burden that has been brought about by Satan, but one which had been brought by Israel on itself. How many of us blame all of our adverse predicaments on the devil, when, sometimes it is just us?

Israel and Judah had been exiled from Jerusalem because of their sins. God kept them in Babylon for 70 years. This was the group that included Shadrach, Meshach, Abednego, and Daniel.

During this period, God raised up a man of extraordinary character named Nehemiah, whose name is translated "Yah comforts" or "Yah encourages." He had held the distinguished position of cupbearer to the king. It was an office of trust: tasting, the king's wine and food. The cupbearer stood between the king and possible death. The fact that Nehemiah, a Jew and a captive, served this Gentile king in such a strategic capacity was an unusual credit and honor.

By the mercy of God, Israel came out of bondage before the seventy years were complete. When they returned to Jerusalem, they did not find it to be the city that they had left. Solomon's grand temple had been destroyed and the walls of the city had been torn down. There was no place to worship and no security. The returning people felt defenseless and vulnerable.

Nehemiah, hearing of the dilapidation of Jerusalem, was so upset that he cried and mourned for days. When is the last time that you cried about somebody else's condition? He sought permission from the king to go to Jerusalem to initiate the rebuilding of the walls. He faced opposition, both from without and from within. It was during this time of opposition that we get the great words of determination that have been repeated by preachers and pastors for centuries:

> ***"I am doing a great work, so that I cannot come down: why should the work cease, whilst I leave it, and come down to you?"***

Nehemiah persevered until the project was complete and the city was fully resettled.

It is important to understand that when Nehemiah arrived in Jerusalem, he found more than just broken walls; he also found broken lives. The only answer for broken lives is the Word of God. One of the reasons that there is so much brokenness among the people of God is that we don't place a priority on hearing the Word of God as we should. In order to bring healing to their brokenness, Nehemiah gathered the people to hear the Word of God.

These people, who had not heard God's standards in a long time, had them renewed in order to establish a standard for living. They were convicted by their wrong-doings. Immediately, remorse set in and repentance began.

Now, the people wept because they saw themselves in light of God's Word and knew that they did not measure up. They knew that they did not deserve to come out of bondage or to be restored to their homeland. Have you ever been under this kind of conviction? It's called "Godly sorrow!"

His response to their feelings of remorse, repentance, and brokenness seemed unusual because he told them to celebrate. It was not the time for sadness. This was a holy or hallowed day, set aside by the Lord, Himself.

I am convinced that any time God lets you know that He loves you despite what He knows you to be, is a day to celebrate. Any time you realize that you have sinned, while the wages of sin is death and you wake up, that is a time to celebrate.

A popular songwriter wrote:

> *"I just want to celebrate another day of living. I just want to celebrate another day of life."*[3]

> *"I just want to celebrate another day of living. I just want to celebrate another day of life."*[4]

---

[3] *"I just Want to Celebrate,"* Written by: Zesses, Hicks/Fekaris, Dino, Lyrics@ EMI Music Publishing, 1965

Things That I Have Seen In God

That songwriter probably wasn't saved, but the Children of Israel could have had those lyrics as their "theme song."

If you are alive on the other side of realizing that you do not deserve to be here, then you ought to celebrate what God has done for you. We can celebrate Jesus.

There are three things about celebration that we all must recognize:

- ✓ Celebration is not without reason. We celebrate what the Lord has done for us. It is a Holy day because it was made by God Who is holy. We should celebrate that God has brought us to *this* day.

- ✓ Celebration is not self-serving. The best way to show that you are excited and appreciative of what God has done for you is by doing something *for* somebody else. In the words of Nehemiah:

> **"Send portions to whom nothing has been prepared."**

---

[4] "*I just Want to Celebrate*," Written by: Zesses, Hicks/Fekaris, Dino, Lyrics@ EMI Music Publishing, 1965

When you realize that you exist because of what has been given to you, give to somebody else.

- ✓ Celebration is not without reason. Celebration is strengthening: *"...the joy of the Lord is your strength."* You want to know what makes you strong of spirit; it is simply the joy of being connected to the Almighty.

I get the sense sometimes that we take our relationships with God for granted, which is why we get weak. My joy of the Lord is not about being happy for what He has done for me, but being excited because He *is* and He is *mine*.

I can shout though I can't pay all of my bills. I can shout though my physical body is not hitting on all cylinders. I can shout even when I don't understand everything that is happening to me. I can shout because *He is*!

Chapter Nine

Resurrection

Live People Carrying Dead Stuff

Luke 7:13-14 (KJV) *And when the Lord saw her, he had compassion on her, and said unto her, Weep not. 14 And he came and touched the bier: and they that bare him stood still. And he said, Young man, I say unto thee, Arise.*

What comes to your mind when you hear the phrase: "Live people carrying dead stuff? I'll bet that you never think about yourself. You probably thought about some other folks that you know.

All of us alive on this planet carry dead stuff. Jesus talked about it when he said that what comes into the mouth cannot contaminate a man because that which contaminates a man comes out and goes into the draught. In other words we eat live stuff and then a healthy body eliminates the waste or that which is dead. If the body ceases to function correctly, that dead stuff will ultimately kill us.

In other words, that which was *life to* me can become *death* to me. That which I took into my system for my good can work against me once it dies. That is what happens in the natural and implies how things work spiritually. Carrying spiritually dead stuff in you can ultimately lead to the death of the carrier.

Unbelief in Jesus Christ can cause your death. Doubting God can cause your death. Bitterness and anger can cause your death.

Nain was a village in southwest Galilee and as Jesus entered the city, crowds of people gathered. Now, we know that everybody who comes to church is not a disciple of the Lord Jesus Christ. Some folks are in the "much people" crowd. They are there for the "gathering".

Things That I Have Seen In God

As Jesus entered the gates of the city a young dead man was being carried out. The fact that he was being carried out tells us that live people were carrying him. I don't mean to be trivial or sarcastic, but dead folks cannot carry dead folks. Someone who could have been doing something else took the time to be bearers of a corpse. To them, there was value in what they were doing.

We can speculate about that young man by suggesting that he died before he had filled his life's potential. Those carrying him could not see that possibility and probably deferred thinking about it because the young man was dead. All they knew was that it was important to remove him from the city before he began to take on the stench of death. The tradition of embalming the dead was not intrinsic to the Jewish tradition, as it was with the Egyptians. Perfumes were used to minimize the odor or smell of death.

Dead bodies were not kept out long and burial often took place within a few hours. Perhaps they feared that keeping the corpse around too long increased the possibility of their catching a disease that might have resulted in *their* deaths. Perhaps burying the dead quickly was part of a tradition with which everyone was familiar. In any case, many gathered to observe the last rites.

The young man's body was removed *before* Jesus came in to the city and this appears to be strange to read in this text. No time had been allocated for Jesus to provide intervention in the situation. He just died and was being carried away for the burial.

What are you trying to eliminate before Jesus has an opportunity to deal with it?

We cannot be too hard on these people, because only one person was really going to be affected by this boy's demise and that was his mother. The only person who would really feel loss was his mother. She was a widow and this was her only son, therefore, she had no source for sustenance. In effect, those, carrying the body for burial, were carrying this woman's last hope for survival.

It is easy to be in a hurry when the "last hope" that you are carrying is not yours. When it's your "last hope," you are subject to say, *"Hold up, is there some other option? Is this the only thing that we can do?"*

There were "much people" of the city who joined with her in the grief that she bore. There will always be more folks willing to help you bury your potential than there will be to encourage you to the possibilities for your future. Don't get "carried away" with the crowd. To do so might cause you to bury something that God wants to resurrect.

Things That I Have Seen In God

There was nowhere in this story where it suggested that the mother or anyone in the crowd knew the identity of Jesus. Neither is it suggested that they were seeking Him. No! He sought them. The folks in Nain were just doing what folks do. We throw away that in which we see no value.

Jesus sees what we cannot see. The Lord saw this woman when she did not see Him. He saw her in her despondency and had compassion on *her*. The text does not say that Jesus had compassion on the young dead man. Jesus showed us, who are to be Christ-like, that Christianity demands that we have compassion on someone other than *ou*r kin or ourselves.

A synonym for the word "compassion" is "mercy." Mercy doesn't ask whose fault it is. Mercy speaks comforting words: "Weep Not!"

Finally, Jesus came and touched the bier or casket. It is important to understand the significance of this act of Jesus. He was not supposed to touch anything that contained a dead person, because it was believed to make a person "ceremonially unclean." One of the reasons given for the priest declining to help the man who had been robbed and beaten and left for "dead" on the Jericho Road was because he was prohibited from touching that which was unclean.

This story, in several ways, reminds me of "me." I didn't always see Him, but thanks to God, He saw me. I may not have become what I wanted to be, but I am what I am and where I am because Jesus saw me. When He saw *me* carrying *my* dead stuff, He had compassion on me. Yes, I was, both the person carrying the dead *and* the dead stuff that was being carried, at the same time.

I was alive - the dead trying to bury the dead - but He touched me.

> *"He touched me. Yes, He touched me, and O, the joy that floods my soul.*
>
> *Something happened and now I know. He touched me and He made me whole."*[5]

The Bible said that it was after the touch of Jesus and his command for the young man to "Get up," that he who was dead sat up and began to speak. Jesus released him to his mother.

He took that which was dead and made it alive again. He took that which was considered useless and made it useful. He can do the same for you.

---

[5] *He Touched Me*, Words and music by William J. Gaither © 1963 Public domain.

Chapter Ten

Nakedness

Naked Came the Stranger

Genesis 3:7 (KJV)
7 And the eyes of them both were opened, and they knew that they were naked; and they sewed fig leaves together, and made themselves aprons.

Things That I Have Seen In God

The word "naked" is defined as "being without clothes" or "nude." More aptly, it is the way in which all of us come into this world. It is also the way that God put Adam and Eve into the Garden of Eden. Gen 2:25 records:

> *"And they were both naked, the man and his wife, and were not ashamed."*

They were as little children, who run naked through a room of adults, but are absolutely unaware of their nakedness. Adam and Eve were not ashamed to appear naked to one another and they were not ashamed to appear before God like that.

This chapter title, "<u>Naked Came the Stranger,</u>[6]" is the title of a movie that I remember, although I don't remember ever seeing the movie. I guess it came to me because of the juxtaposition of the two words "naked" and "stranger." You must admit that something is amiss when you see a stranger (someone with whom you have absolutely no relationship) naked.

I thought about how Adam and Eve felt the first time that they saw themselves after eating that fruit. They saw themselves differently than they had ever seen themselves. It is like losing your virginity, whether you are a male or female; once it is done, it is

---

[6] Harvey Anderson (novel) Jake Barnes (screenplay) <u>Naked Came the Stranger,</u> 1975 Radley Metzger, Director, Catalyst Productions

done. Married or unmarried, you cannot take it back. You see yourself differently going forward.

What Adam and Eve saw in the mirror, they had never seen. They saw strangers in the mirror, but the strangers were themselves. What an awestruck moment it must be to see yourself naked for the first time in your life. What anxiety one must cope with to realize that you have to do something about something that was never a problem?

Adam and Eve ate from the one tree in the Garden that God had forbidden. They partook of the accursed thing. The death that God told them would result from eating from that tree had begun to take hold. Their deaths were the same way as of the cursed fig tree. It began at the root. They were dying, but they could not see the physical manifestations of that death.

The death started in their spirits and in their minds, as they began to see what God said was good, in their flesh, had turned "bad." They became ashamed of what God had made. What Adam and Eve saw in their minds was the manifestation of what was going on in their spirits. They saw that they were not covered by God anymore. They saw that they were disconnected from God.

Sin still disconnects us from our covering.

Your child does not come into the house and greet you the same way when he or she brings a bad report card home.

The bad part is that Adam and Eve lost their Godliness, but the good part is that they had not lost their God consciousness. It is God consciousness that causes shame. It is God consciousness that ultimately causes Godly sorrow which will lead to repentance.

They were naked and ashamed. That is precisely the way anyone who sins should see himself. God beholds the evil and the good.

God saw Eve when she talked with the serpent. He saw Adam standing there and failing to exercise his responsibility as her covering. He sensed Eve's changed appetite from the fruit of that forbidden tree. He saw Eve eat the fruit and give a portion to Adam. Why didn't God intervene? Why didn't God do something? He already had. He had given them His word.

God beholds us when we sin. I do not know where we think God is when we think those crazy thoughts that we think. All of us are naked before God. We have sinned and come short of His glory. We might be saved, but we are stilled marred while we are in the Master's hands. On our best dressed day, our sins are laid bare before God. So then, the question is, "What should I do when I realize that I am naked?

First, don't seek carnal covering. Adam and Eve sought carnal covering for their calamity in their confusion.

Both Adam and Eve came to realize the awesome price of having sin to dwell in your spirit. They realized that to do that, you only lose fellowship with God. There is no fellowship between darkness and light. Their responses were the same as anyone who knows that he is naked and ashamed of what he is seeing – sin. They seek to cover what is naked and since they were thinking carnally, they sought carnal covering.

We tend to do the same thing. We will mess up and then try to find someone who will go along with what we have done. They cannot restore us to where we have fallen nor make the situation any better. They just make us feel better.

We will get the same result as Adam and Eve. We think that we are covered, while the shame of our nakedness still appears to the only one that can cover us – God.

Secondly, don't hide from your help. That's exactly what Adam and Eve did. They hid from their help. Adam said,

"I heard your voice and I was afraid."

This is Adam's Creator. Everything that he had, God gave it to him. He gave him food to eat, a wife, a place to live, and dominion over everything that had been created. This is the same God that Adam talked with daily and to whom Adam had never lied, yet, Adam feared Him.

Life is really messed up when you start to fear the one with whom you should anticipate having fellowship. Sin will do that to you. Once fear sets in, the natural thing to do is to hide from the one that you fear. Eve talked to the one that she should have feared and both she and Adam hid from the One with whom they should have had conversation.

How many of us talk with the devil daily and then hide from, or should I say, attempt to hide from God? Folks "hide" in liquor bottles and on drugs, while others "hide" in attitudes that do them no good.

When we hide from God, we are hiding from the only one that can help us. God sees all and knows all. He knows that we are but dust. The truth is He knew we were going to mess up *before* we messed up. He is not coming to harm us but to help us. If God had wanted to harm Adam and Eve, He could have done that without coming into the garden.

Thirdly, don't accuse the Almighty. Adam and Eve played the blame game.

> *"And the man said, the woman whom thou gavest to be with me, she gave me of the tree, and I did eat. 13 And*

> *the LORD God said unto the woman, What is this that thou hast done? And the woman said, the Serpent beguiled me, and I did eat."*

Look at what happened here. First, the brother blamed what happened on the woman that God gave him. Secondly, Eve blamed what happened on the serpent that God had created and put in the garden. They both played this blame game that we all play. The comedian, Flip Wilson, used to say: *"The devil made me do it"*. We say the same thing, except we might say "the devil in the blue dress" or "that demon with the big chest." They indicted themselves with the same three words, "*I did eat.*"

Eve did not make Adam eat and the serpent did not make Eve eat. Not only that, but Eve didn't have the power to make Adam eat and the serpent didn't have the power to make Eve eat. They ate of their own accord. They compromised the submission that they had to God.

"STOP BLAMING GOD!" The covering that Adam selected was carnal and cost very little. It was a fig leaf. The covering that God provided was from an animal, costing the life of the animal. The animal was faultless, while both Adam and Eve were guilty. That which was without sin had to die so that the sinful could be covered. Blood had to be shed.

Finally, we must seek the One who can help you find the way back. That which had been friendly to Adam and Eve, would now become their enemies. The ground that they had dominated would now bring forth thorns and thistles. The animals that Adam had the privilege of naming would revolt against him. Doing that which God had given them to do as a charge, "be fruitful and multiply," would become painful and laborious. Adam and Eve were kicked out of the only home that they had ever known, the Garden of Eden. To put it simply, they lost! Satan had tricked them into state of "lostness."

This story would be tragic if it ended this way. This account of Scripture would be sorrowful, if it ended with Adam and Eve being covered, but kicked out for good.

> *"And he placed at the east of the garden of Eden Cherubims, and a flaming sword which turned every way, to keep the way of the tree of life."*

God set an angel there *not* to keep Adam and Eve from ever getting back, but to make sure that there would always be a *way* back. Regardless of what you have done, there is always a way back.

Christ is the One whose blood is sufficient to cover all of our sins. He is the one whose life is sufficient to cover all of our nakedness.

Chapter Eleven

Beauty

What are you looking at?

Gen 3:6 *"And when the woman saw that the tree was good for food, and that it was pleasant to the eyes, and a tree to be desired to make one wise, she took of the fruit thereof, and did eat, and gave also unto her husband with her; and he did eat."*

Things That I Have Seen In God

It is amazing how two or three people or any number of people can see the same thing and yet come away with different descriptions of what they saw.

I know that I am right about that, because I like television shows about law and justice where witnesses, who saw the same event are interviewed and tell what they saw differently. When the hearts and the motivation of two different people see the same thing, one can come away with the truth about what he saw and the other can come away with a lie.

Two parents, who come upon their children in an altercation, can both see the other person's son as having started the altercation, but *only* one of them could have been the "starter." The other child would have had to be the "escalator."

Two people, seeing a woman inadvertently drop a one hundred dollar bill from her purse could view the same event differently. One could see it as a "blessing" from God for them; the other could see it as an opportunity to witness and minister to this woman after returning her money.

Have you ever seen something that some friend of yours thought was the "bomb?" Your friend may have described it as something "to die for," but you saw absolutely no value in it. They thought it was beautiful and you thought that it was the ugliest thing you had ever seen.

Either of the two parties, seeing the same thing so differently, could ask, *"What were you looking at?"*

In the Bible, the synoptic gospel writers, Matthew, Mark, and Luke, tell the story of Jesus from different perspectives, revealing different facts about what they saw. In the case of these observers and historians, the truth was told from different perspectives, but, for many others, it is not the truth, but falsehoods.

Everybody makes choices. We are born choosing to either drink the milk our mother provides or turn our heads. Most of us are either victors or victims of our own choices.

Choice is the first thing that God gave man. We have defined and described the power and privilege of choice as "free moral agency." With the privilege of choice comes the responsibility to choose correctly. This power to choose correctly comes from acquiring the necessary information and having the good sense and courage to make the right choices. Choices are the external indicators of our internal motivations.

All of us have the right to choose what we will, but none of us can change what is at the end of the road that we choose. We have the choice of life and good or death and evil. God has set this choice before us. Each of us is given the opportunity to live by God's System, but we can choose to live by the world's system. How does a saint live in this world that is so anti-God and abide by God's System?

Satan, our great adversary, knows that we cannot live by God's System looking at the circumstances. That is why he attempts to trap us by having us focus on being relevant. I think that the current term is, "keeping it real."

When you look at the circumstances of the world you are going to see other people doing what God has told us not to do. Not only are you going to see unsaved people involving themselves in behaviors that God prohibited, but you are going to see church folks that we respect, involved in about everything imaginable.

That which God says is bad has been deemed as good by many of our "leaders" and "mentors." I'm just going to leave that there. I could talk about some of the so-called Christian movies or the mode of dress of some our gospel performers.

God created everything by the power of His Word. John 1:1-3 (KJV) records:

> *"In the beginning was the Word, and the Word was with God, and the Word was God.*
> *2 The same was in the beginning with God.*
> *3 All things were made by him; and without him was not any thing made that was made."*

Things That I Have Seen In God

God created the sun and the moon. He provided both our daytimes and nighttimes. He created the fish for the seas, the fowls of the air, and every creeping thing upon the earth. He put His own image in the earth with the creation of man.

Man was placed in the earth to be a reflection of God in the earth. Man's assignment was to exercise dominion over his environment and charged them:

> *"Be fruitful, and multiply, and replenish the earth, and subdue it: and have dominion over the fish of the sea, and over the fowl of the air, and over every living thing that moveth upon the earth."*

Man's purposes for being were to guide, guard, and govern his assigned area of responsibility. That's the same thing that we are supposed to do. You may not have a garden, but you have a house, or an apartment. There is an assigned area of responsibility in your personal life and in your ministry with the church.

God provided everything for Adam with only one stipulation: He could eat from all of the trees in the garden, except the one that was known as the *"tree of knowledge of good and evil."* The penalty for doing so was death.

Finally, the last piece in the garden was Eve.

Eve was described as the "help" that was right for Adam. She was bone of his bone and flesh of his flesh.

It is to Eve that Satan came and, in his subtlety, suggested at least three things:

- ✓ That God had lied to Adam when He told them they would die as a result of eating from the forbidden tree.
- ✓ That God was withholding the status of "god" from both she and Adam.
- ✓ That God was trying to deprive them of the privileges that He had.

Let's examine the scenario chronologically:

1. Eve saw the tree as good for food.
2. Eve saw the tree as pleasant to the eyes.
3. Eve saw the tree as desirable to make one wise.
4. Eve took of the fruit.
5. Eve ate.
6. Eve gave her husband.
7. Adam ate.

According to Bible commentator and pastor John McArthur, Eve's deception took three forms:

Things That I Have Seen In God

1) The tree was good for food appealing to her physical appetite.

2) It was pleasant to the eye, thereby, exciting her emotional appetite.

3) The tree was good to make one wise and provoked her intellectual appetite.

Here are: the lust of the flesh (food), the lust of eyes (eye candy), and the pride of life (knowledge). Many of our troubles can be tracked back to our veracious appetites. They include: physical problems, such as diabetes, high blood pressure, indebtedness caused by the desire to have what we don't need, and sexual issues.

Nothing was really lost until Adam ate because he was the carrier of the seed that would get contaminated by sin in his body. What we must consider is the great *influence* that Eve exercised on Adam. It does not excuse him, but it indicts her. Eve developed an appetite for "arsenic," "strychnine," or "snake venom."

Actually, it indicts anyone who is not in charge but uses his influence to move the one who is in charge away from what God has ordained.

If we examine several of the mistakes made by

Eve, we may be able to stem our own appetites for the ungodly. We may be able to fend off the one who came to Eve's door and who will surely show up at your door. It is not *if*, but when. The Bible says:

"Resist the devil and he will flee from you."

We would not have to resist him, if he were not coming.

First, Eve gave Satan place in her life, respecting his deceptive status by lending him her ear. Eph 4:27: Paul writes in Ephesians 4:27:

"…nor give place to the devil."

Secondly, she gave Satan a base of operation in her life. She opened a door and Satan entered. She elevated him to a place equal with that of God in her life. How many of us have opened doors to the enemy? The only Spiritual Being that is authorized to speak into our lives is God. She allowed a corrupting influence into her life. Filthy communications corrupt good morals. Eve allowed Satan to speak into her life about what was right and wrong. She did not know or she ignored the fact that she was operating out of her purpose. She should have told Satan to talk with her covering.

Finally, Eve opted to walk by what *she saw* as opposed to what God had said. This is not so much about a man and his wife as it is about the covering of a household or family. Adam represents her covering, with the responsibility of providing for and protecting his wife. God is God of order and He spoke to Adam, who had the covering for his wife.

I would hope that Adam passed on to Eve in great detail everything that God had said about the tree of knowledge of good and evil and that Eve had believed him. Therefore, Eve had the choice to either *walk by faith* in what she knew God had said or to *walk by* what she saw.

We must also assume that she knew or God would have punished her wrongfully with the pain of child birth. She willfully, chose to walk by sight. Eve saw that which God described as leading to death as good for life-sustaining food. Anytime it seems that which God says is bad as being good, we are heading for trouble. Our sins will find us out. She saw that which was good for nothing as good for nourishment.

Death is the end of the ultimate weakness of man. The inability to sustain our life any further is our ultimate weakness. She saw that which God said would make man weak unto death as good for life. She saw a more abundant life in that which God said would only lead to death.

One conversation with Satan caused this woman to change her whole perspective. One conversation with "ole slew foot" caused Eve to stop seeing things God's way and to seeing them Satan's way. One conversation with the enemy caused Eve to stop seeing things from a holy perspective and begin to see those same things from the perspective of the devil.

How many times have you changed perspective? How much are you seeing from the perspective of the world as opposed to the perspective of God?

If a man is a friend of this world's system, he is an enemy of God. Some of us are friends of God in some areas and, by our behaviors, enemies of God in other areas?

Eve bought a bill of goods. Satan sold her on the lust for something that she either already had or was certain to receive. Adam and Eve were in charge of everything that existed at that time, so they were already [little "g"] gods. They were guiding, guarding, and governing their environment in the same way that God guides, guards, and governs His environment. They only had to answer to God.

Satan is a deceiver. He was not trying to advance their status. He was trying to steal their glory. Satan has been called the "god of this world." How do you think that he got that status? He got it when Adam lost it. By deceiving us into thinking that God is withholding something from us he is trying to get us to forfeit our status.

As the Second Adam, Jesus has restored all of us to the status that Adam and Eve had in the garden. If God gave His only begotten Son, how will he not freely give us all things?

We have dominion!

We have authority!

We have signs following us!

All that we have to do to maintain our status is keep on seeing everything the way that God sees them.

"YOU HAVE TO BE VERY CAREFUL ABOUT ALLOWING SOMEONE ELSE TO SPEAK INTO YOUR LIFE, DEVELOPING *YOUR* LIFE PLAN, BASED ON SOME ENTITY OPERATING ON BAD INFORMATION."

Chapter Twelve

Father!

Happy Father's Day!

Malachi 1:6-9 (KJV)
6 A son honoureth his father, and a servant his master: if then I be a father, where is mine honour? and if I be a master, where is my fear? saith the LORD of hosts unto you, O priests, that despise my name. And ye say, Wherein have we despised thy name?
7 Ye offer polluted bread upon mine altar; and ye say, Wherein have we polluted thee? In that ye say, The table of the LORD is contemptible.
8 And if ye offer the blind for sacrifice, is it not evil? and if ye offer the lame and sick, is it not evil? offer it now unto thy governor; will he be pleased with thee, or accept thy person? saith the LORD of hosts.
9 And now, I pray you, beseech God that he will be gracious unto us: this hath been by your means: will he regard your persons? saith the LORD of hosts.

1 Corinthians 4:15 (KJV)
15 For though ye have ten thousand instructors in Christ, yet have ye not many fathers: for in Christ Jesus I have begotten you through the gospel.

The greeting, Happy Father's Day," is like many that we hear throughout the year. "Merry Christmas", "Happy New Year", "Happy Mother's Day", and "Happy Birthday" are included in the myriad of salutations that permeate our existence. Many of us have uttered these words to somebody and many of us have heard them. The question is not whether we have heard them, but whether we appreciate their meanings.

Do these words have *real* meaning? Are they the "appropriate" sayings for the day, like "Good Morning," or are they substantive?

When we utter the words "Happy Father's Day," are we seriously wishing the person happiness? I am sure that we should be wishing them happiness for *that* day, but how can we do that, if we have not done anything to contribute to that happiness? It's like beating your wife last night and then waking up and saying, "Good Morning" which suggests that you want them to have a good day! It rings hollow!

The book of Malachi, the last book in the Old Testament, deals with how God feels about disobedient people who have given Him less than what He required. It gives us a parting glimpse of how the "Last Days Revival" will look. Malachi 4:6:

> **"And he shall turn the heart of the fathers to the children, and the heart of the children to their fathers, lest I come and smite the earth with a curse."**

There will be a return to fidelity in covenant relationships.

Luke 1:17 records,

> *"And he shall go before him in the spirit and power of Elias, to turn the hearts of the fathers to the children, and the disobedient to the wisdom of the just; to make ready a people prepared for the Lord."*

God takes issue with a people who call Him Father because the other half of the privilege of calling someone father is that you have to be his child. You have to be His child, not just in word, but in deed. Whoever calls Him "Father," must honor Him. A son honors his father. What you do must be in line with what you are calling Him.

The primary issue which is addressed is the offering, but the issue is much larger - the covenant requirement of God to bring the best. The people who had agreed to the covenant requirements of God in order to get the benefits of being in covenant with Him, decided that God required too much. While they wished Him "Happy Father's Day," they despised keeping covenant with Him.

The people were doing "devilment" and "devilment" always gives you another parentage. There was a religious group that slipped up to Jesus, declaring to Him that Abraham was their *father* and that they had never been in bondage to any man. They ignored the relationship between God and Jesus Christ and, thereby, dishonored God. I contend that those in that crowd were "confused."

How many people are confused today? While they are saying, "Happy Father's Day" to God, they are actually serving another God by not honoring Him and reverencing Him. You have to be very careful about allowing someone else to speak into your life, developing your life plan based on the commentary of some entity operating on bad information.

Paul spoke to a people who had "divided parentage." It was the same issue with this Corinthian Church that God had with His people in Malachi. They were trying to hear and respond to multiple voices and had become "confused" about what direction they should move. As Israel was in Elijah's day, they were halted between two opinions. It was like having a "Father's Day" gift and not knowing to whom to give it because you cannot distinguish who your father is.

Paul called the church's attention to the divisions that had been created, as they tried to establish their allegiances to Paul, Apollos, Cephas, and of Christ.

Everybody is not a "father." What is natural proves this point. Ask yourself, "aren't there a whole lot more sons, brothers, and cousins than there are fathers?" Aren't there a whole lot less people fathering children than there are sperm donors? A fifteen year old can be a sperm donor, but I doubt that he can be much of a father.

Paul juxtapositions two things: instructors and fathers. This juxtaposition of these two entities would not make any sense at all, unless there was some confusion about who was a father. If someone is confused about whom a father is, they could end up honoring a non-father and dishonoring a father.

There are a whole lot more spiritual instructors than there are spiritual fathers in a person's life. Fathers do not just sow seeds, but they remove weeds which can suck the life out of what they have sown. Fathers pluck them out so that those seedlings can come up. They pray for the seeds that they have sown and that God will watch when they are not around to watch.

I'm referring to the father's children. It does not matter whether it's God our Father, our spiritual father, or our physical father. They all do the same thing. One commentator said that the spirit of God's minister is that of a fatherly spirit, not that of an instructor's spirit.

The "instructor" of (paidagōgous) in Paul's day

was a trusted slave who was placed in complete charge of a child's welfare and growth until he was grown. He was even in charge of escorting the child to school and seeing that no harm came to him. He was employed by the child's father.

The Corinthian church had an unlimited number of capable instructors and teachers, but only one "spiritual father." All of us have had mentors, peers, and wise friends who have spoken wisdom into our lives and caused us to prosper. These persons could be easily mistaken for our parents.

Paul was very definitive in his exposition on this matter:

> "I am not the only one that has ever spoken wisdom into your live"!
>
> "I am not the only one that has ever laid hands on you"!
>
> "I am not the only one that is responsible for the spiritual success that you are experiencing, yet, I am your only father."

Paul raised the issue of overall care and concern, suggested that, as their father, he cares beyond all of their other instructors. He was the one who had brought these people to Christ Jesus that they might receive life. He had given birth to this church and overseeing the growth of this church.

Imitate the *right* person.

"Wherefore I beseech you, be ye followers of me."

The Greek word for our English word "followers" (mimētai ginesthe) means imitators. Every father should live such a life that his children could follow in his steps.

1 Corinthians 11:1:

"Be ye followers of me, even as I also am of Christ."

When you understand that Christ is God and God is our Father, you will understand how Paul became a father. Paul told this church to imitate his fatherhood as he has imitated the fatherhood of God. They cannot become a father, imitating one of the many instructors that you come in contact with in life. Your destiny in God can be destroyed by following the wrong leader.

This teaching was not about him getting more honor than he deserved, but it was about the danger that they could have experienced in missing out on what they can become. If the Corinthian Church imitated Paul, and if Paul imitated Christ, and if Jesus the Son imitated God the Father, then the Corinthian Church would ultimately be imitating God.

Perhaps there should be more "imitators" in

the body of Christ. God is Jehovah-Rophe – The Lord that Heals. Jesus laid hands on the sick and they recovered. Paul laid hands on the sick and they recovered. We ought to imitate them.

God is the "resurrector." Jesus is the Resurrection who resurrected three people. Paul resurrected a man that fell from the balcony at one of his sermons and died. We ought to imitate them.

A father is honored when his children take what he has taught them and applies it to their lives. In other words, his children imitate him.

I am a "copycat!" I am not trying to be an "original." If it was good enough for Jesus, it is good enough for me.

Chapter Thirteen

Responsibility!

The Buck Stops Here!

1 Kings 18:21 (KJV)
21 And Elijah came unto all the people, and said, How long halt ye between two opinions? if the LORD be God, follow him: but if Baal, then follow him. And the people answered him not a word.

When someone says, "The Buck Stops Here"[7], they normally mean that what other people have been passing along as not their job and have been using one excuse after another to get out of doing will not be passed any further. They are saying that they will take the responsibility for what needs to happen and get it done.

What I want to look at is the other side of this. I want to look at the "buck" as the "prosperity" of a person, a family, a church, or a nation. I define prosperity, not as "money" or "wealth," per se, but as the ability to go forward in the things of God. It is the ability to pursue your destiny. In this particular sense, I see the statement as the place where prosperity grinds to a standstill. It signifies the place where what is supposed to be moving comes to a complete halt.

This is the life of many believers who are supposed to be, by definition, "more than conquerors." It is the life of many of us who are supposed to be going from victory to victory. We are not going any place! We are halted and what halts us is not something that we cannot do anything about. It is not the enemy overpowering a significantly weaker church, but it is more like a significantly stronger church overpowering itself. When the buck stops in the life of a Kingdom person, Kingdom family,

---

[7] President Harry S. Truman

kingdom church or Kingdom nation, it is because of indecision.

The king of record is Ahab. Ahab was appointed king of the ten tribes, based north of Judah. He has a "famous wife" who was named Jezebel.

Jezebel is a Persian name meaning, "Where is the prince?" It is perhaps derived from its Phoenician name meaning, "Baal is the prince." As the wife of King Ahab of Israel, she was allowed by Ahab to bring the worship of Baal from Sidon, where her father Ethbaal was king. Not only did Jezebel introduce Baal worship to the people of God, but she also tried to destroy all of God's prophets.

There can be no Jezebel without an Ahab. He was responsible for all that Jezebel did. Without Ahab's cooperation, all that Jezebel had was the desire to rule wickedly.

Because of Ahab's wicked rule, God turned nature against the nation and it did not rain for three and a half years. It was not all Ahab's fault. The people of God, who had read the "Ten Commandments and knew that they should have no other gods other than Jehovah, chose to become multi-theistic. They moved from reserving their worship for Jehovah only to believing that they could also worship Baal.

Israel was guilty of a "divided heart." They sought to serve two masters. Like many saints, they had divided loyalties. On the one hand we might serve God, but we might also seek to be a "friend of this world's system." John said that if any man is a friend of this world, (this world's system) he is an enemy of God. He knew that the God of this world's system is Satan.

After three years of seclusion, first at the Brook Cherith, where ravens brought him bread and meat, and secondly, at the Widow of Zarephath's home, where he existed off a barrel of meal and a cruse of oil that God supernaturally elongated, God sent Elijah a Word.

After Elijah resurrected the widow's son that had died, God directed him to appear before Ahab. God gave the prophet a Word and the prophet responded. He wasn't too attached to the brook to leave it when God told him to go to Zarephath; and he was not too attached to the widow and her son, when God told him to show himself to Ahab. When you are on assignment from the Lord, you cannot get too attached to the ground that you are passing through. Your attachment has to be to the God of that ground.

Ahab, after giving Elijah an audience, asked whether he was the one who had "troubled Israel."

You cannot serve God effectively unless you are ready to deal with false accusations. One of Satan's names is "the accuser of the brethren."

Elijah responded to the accusation by declaring that it was the king and his household that had reneged on the commandments of God and that his assignment was to straighten it all out.

In order to accomplish that, he told Ahab to gather all of the prophets, including the prophets of Baal, to a certain place. Every prophet, who had "subsisted at Jezebel's table, was summoned. It should be noted that Elijah did not even call the king's table his table. He called it "Jezebel's table."

Once there, Elijah addresses the people of God with a question: "How long halt ye between two opinions?" The people gave no response. There are at least three things that can be learned from this: First, your indecision can do to you what Satan cannot. Indecision can stop you!

Some of the other versions say:

"How long will you falter between two opinions?" (NKJV)

"How long will you go limping with two different opinions?" (NRSV)

"How long will you try to have it both ways?" (GW)

"How long are you going to sit on the fence?" (MSG)

The issues of the question are being halted, faltering, limping, trying to have it both ways, or sitting on the fence.

Satan cannot stop us, but if he can bind up our mind with indecision about who God is, we will grind ourselves to a halt. Many of our country's problems are about the failure to decide who God is! We have become multi-theistic as a nation. We have created a "culture" where there is great indecision about who God is. Even our seminaries have questions about who God really is! Many church-goers have become multi-theistic.

We indicate who our God is by our behavior. It is how we live every day and the decisions that we make. It is who we allow to govern our lives. One of the greatest indicators of indecision in a Christian's mind about God is carnal behavior.

Secondly, no interruption can stay beyond your decision.

Elijah said that Israel was halted by indecision. That was all that it was. *"You are off track. You have run aground and you cannot go forward until you get back on track."*

Things That I Have Seen In God

What does it take to get back on track? All that it takes is to start doing what they stopped doing--making a decision! They had to decide: Is it Jehovah God or is it Baal God?

In our case, it might be a decision between what the world says I should forgive and what God says I should forgive. It might be a decision about whether or not to play the lottery. It could be a decision of whether or not to do what God says is right or to follow the footsteps of my peers.

Jesus referred to people who vacillate between being "hot" and "cold" as good for nothing. These were people who thought that they had it religiously "going on," but Jesus said that He was on the outside trying to get in.

Thirdly, no intelligent decision can be made until you start thinking for yourself. Baal, the god of fertility, could do nothing once God stopped the rain.

Actually, Baal could do nothing *before* God stopped the rain; he was "perpetrating."

The question of Elijah was: "Now that you have seen the power of the One True and Living God, will you move forward or remain stuck in indecision? Now that you are no longer up under the influence of

Jezebel, what will you decide?"

Baal proved himself impotent and God proved Himself to be El-Shaddai. This was an exclamation point! All of us have Godly exclamation points in our lives. That is a, "Yeah, I really am God" point!

This was a, "If all that I have done has not convinced you that I am God, then watch this" moment!

It is designed to wake us up so that we can make an intelligent decision about who God is and what place He holds in our lives!

Chapter Fourteen

Houses

The Legacy of an Empty House!

Luke 11:24-26 (KJV)
24 When the unclean spirit is gone out of a man, he walketh through dry places, seeking rest; and finding none, he saith, I will return unto my house whence I came out.
25 And when he cometh, he findeth it swept and garnished.
26 Then goeth he, and taketh to him seven other spirits more wicked than himself; and they enter in, and dwell there: and the last state of that man is worse than the first.

Luke 11:24-26 (NKJV)
24 "When an unclean spirit goes out of a man, he goes through dry places, seeking rest; and finding none, he says, 'I will return to my house from which I came.'
25 "And when he comes, he finds it swept and put in order.
26 "Then he goes and takes with him seven other spirits more wicked than himself, and they enter and dwell there; and the last state of that man is worse than the first."

I recently watched a segment of the television show "Law and Order." In this episode, Robin Williams was a suspected offender. During his cross examination, he stated that he had never been arrested. The District Attorney pounced on him and asked him, *"Weren't you arrested as a teen for burning down an abandoned house?"* To this, he stated that he burned it down because some boys in the neighborhood were using the house as a drug hang out.

When asked why he didn't report it to the police, he replied that he had, but the Police Chief's son was one of the ring leaders and no one would believe him; so the police did nothing.

There are several truths here: One is that what this house became and was used for had to do with who inhabited it. Secondly, the house gained its reputation (Drug House) by the activities of its inhabitants. Thirdly, the house suffered the consequences of who had inhabited it. Lastly, even though the house had nothing to do with who had inhabited it, the house was burned down because the police did not choose to deal with the inhabitants.

I have seen many empty houses that have been mistreated and ill-cared for by their previous owners liberated by a "vacate notice" or "eviction notice." You have too! Once these units are vacated, they are at the mercy of whoever occupies them next. They can become as opulent as a palace or as broken down as a shanty. It has everything to do with who inhabits the empty house next and where their priorities lay.

1 Corinthians 6:19:

> *"What? know ye not that your body is the temple of the Holy Ghost which is in you, which ye have of God, and ye are not your own?"*

The <u>Message Bible</u> calls the body "a sacred place."

Jesus exorcised a demon from a man who could not speak. Some folks attributed the powers that Jesus had to the devil. Most pagan exorcists sought to remove demons by magical incantations. Rabbis in the second century still accused Jesus and Jewish Christians of using sorcery to achieve the miracles he performed.

Jesus exposed the absurdity of this idea by telling his protagonists that a kingdom divided against itself would not continue to exist. Why would God's people fight Godliness?

Jesus, the Lawyer of Lawyers, took His argument to the next level by explaining that it takes a stronger man to kick out a man that is strong, armed, and barricaded in his house. In the illustration, the "strong man" was "Satan." The place that "Satan" called his house was the life of someone. The one who kicked "Satan-the strong man" out was

Jesus.

> <u>The Message Bible</u> records it like this,:
>
> *"This is war, and there is no neutral ground. If you're not on my side, you're the enemy. If you're not helping, you're making things worse".*

To further illustrate the danger of attempting to be neutral about Him, Jesus explained what can happen to such people. Unfilled and complacent people are easy targets for Satan.

Unclean spirits can come out. The Lord exorcised this demon. The desert was believed to be the habitation of demons because demons need a resting place (that is, someone or something living that they can enter and torment). This demon sought a house to inhabit.

Secondly, a "torn up life" can be put in order. A life can be put as God had intended for it to be in the first place. When God created the world, He created an orderly universe. Disorder came with the entrance of sin. Sin got in through the open door that Adam opened. Satan is the author of confusion. God is the author of order.

Whatever God has Satan wants. The Bible records that on "the seventh day," God rested. Satan wants rest too. He wants a counterfeit rest. The problem is that Satan has no semblance of rest without a body. Like the demons that were exorcised from the demoniac of Gadara, he needs something with hands and feet.

Jesus was talking to people who thought that they were Believers. Satan was seeking another person among the worshipers to inhabit, but could not find an open door in anybody's life. So, he reconsidered the life he left.

Satan will always reconsider the saved. Jesus, suggested that our spiritual destiny depends on our making a decision about Him. Being delivered from one force does not necessarily mean that you have embraced another force. Just because you have been delivered from the strong man by a stronger man does not mean that you have embraced the "Deliverer." Let me be even plainer still! A whole lot of people who have embraced Jesus as Savior have not embraced Him as Lord.

In the demon's absence, the home (the person's life) had been swept and made clean, but it was still empty. In fact, the accommodations were now so inviting that the demon found seven other spirits more evil than itself, and they all entered the person and lived there. The demon returned to the person it came from, but he did not return alone.

Satan will return to find out whether we were seeking to be delivered from our afflictions or had chosen to embrace the God of our deliverance.

Satan is not stronger than God, but he is stronger than the one who does not have God dwelling in him. Being delivered from whatever does not give us the strength to deal with what we were delivered from. The one that has been delivered can *feel* stronger because he is no longer under the effects of whatever was affecting him. When a person catches the flu, they are weakened by that influenza virus. Once they have recovered from the flu, they will usually feel stronger because they are no longer affected by the flu's symptoms.

The reality is that they are no stronger than they were *before* they caught the flu the first time and they can become more susceptible to catching it again. The strength that they felt from getting over the flu could have been misleading.

Jesus illustrated two unfortunate human tendencies: the personal desire to reform, that often does not last long, and the attempts to take care of life in disaster. It is not enough to be emptied of evil; the person must, then, be filled with the power of the Holy Spirit to accomplish God's new purpose in his life.

This story could be your story and it could have a different ending. It could read that the last state of the man was better than the first. It was better because once he received the power to choose correctly, he chose Jesus. Though he was like the prodigal and had lost all that he had - his fellowship with his father, his financial security, and his friends - he came to himself. When you come to yourself, you have the power to choose what you, heretofore, have not chosen.

Have you ever been this man? I have. I have been this man—*"sinking deep in sin, far from the peaceful shore, very deeply stained within, sinking to rise no more...."*[8]

I have been this man. I have had the Master of the sea hear *"my despairing cry, and from the waters lifted me,"* so that I can sing out, "Safe am I."

That will make you shout, but that is not enough. It is not enough to shout and be empty. It is not enough to shout and continue to be conformed to this world. It is not enough to shout and forsake transformation. It is not enough to shout and then not present your body as a living sacrifice. It is not enough to be empty-spirited.

We must cry out with a voice of triumph:

"Bread of Heaven, Bread of Heaven, feed me till I want no more!"

---

[8] James Rowe, Howard Smith, *Love Lifted Me*, 1912

Things That I Have Seen In God